SHAI

Educated in the US and UK, Philip Brebner was awarded a PhD from Glasgow University for his thesis on the political history of urban planning and architecture in Algeria 1830 to 1982. After lecturing at architecture schools in Jeddah and Porto, his first novel, *A Country of Vanished Dreams,* was published by Picador to critical acclaim, and translated. As well as fiction, he has published in academic journals and the Independent. To keep the wolf from the door, he taught creative writing for the British Council and dealt in rare rugs and textiles in Istanbul. He now divides his time between Portugal and Morocco, the inspiration for the previous novel in the Ramzi series, *Shadows of Marrakech.*

By the same author

A COUNTRY OF VANISHED DREAMS

THE FABULOUS ROAD

LIGHTER THAN AIR

FADO

SHADOWS OF MARRAKECH

Author website: www.philipbrebner.com

First published 2022 by Thames Street Press,
Oxford

ISBN: 978-1-9196075-2-8

Design: www.lrbcreative.com

SHADOWS OF ESSAOUIRA

Philip Brebner

THAMES STREET PRESS
OXFORD

SHADOWS OF ESSAOUIRA

ONE

Long before dawn, Ramzi woke to the screech of gulls and pounding of the Atlantic. Plumping the pillows, he stretched across the brass bed, relishing the sulphurous scent of sea. How exotic he thought Essaouira in contrast to Marrakech—straight after stepping off the bus the day before, he found the port's palette of white and blue, thundering breezes and strange phosphorescence a tonic to the torpor of Morocco's red desert city in summer.

Then, amid the squeals and squawks, a small scream. Human. Throwing back the sheets, Ramzi pulled on jeans and a T-shirt, opened the door, peering onto the landing.

A lamp was on and a woman stood there, fear on her face.

'Are you okay? I thought I heard someone cry out?'

She handed across a small square of paper.

'A *jidwel*.'

Ramzi looked at the pen marks. A Star of David, with Hebrew inscriptions in the six triangles and in the middle. Blood was sprinkled across it.

'My name,' she said, pointing to the hexagon in the centre. 'This is a *shour*. A spell.'

Ramzi knew this fell between black magic and witchcraft. It was a form of evil that may be anywhere anytime, in a rock, or a palm grove, an item of clothing or in henna used to dye women's hair. Both Moroccan Muslims and Jews shared a trust in its power.

'Do you believe it?'

'I don't know. My Moroccan grandmother told me about them. She and my grandfather's families emigrated to Israel from Meknès and here in Essaouira. One story was about a cousin who didn't like the choice of her son's wife, so she visited a *sahir*.'

'A sorcerer?'

'Yes, and hid a *shour* this in their apartment. The couple started to quarrel day and night, which they had never done before. Finally, they brought in a Rabbi who did a search of their rooms and discovered a *jidwel*, a piece of paper like this. He wrote another to break the spell, and from then on the couple lived in wedded bliss.'

'Are you worried about your marriage?'
'No—my life.'
Stepping back, she shut the door.

TWO

Ramzi had spent the summer at Riad Waqi, the traditional courtyard house he owned and ran as a guest house in Marrakech. Brutally, September brought little relief from the oily heat of August and this, coupled with the Hen Party from Hell, tipped him over the edge. Normally he declined both hen and stag parties, which could disturb the neighbours in their quiet alleyway in the historic medina. However, the initial enquiry from Ryan seemed for a group of friends or family. Only on arrival did they discover the five rooms would be shared by ten women, nine wearing 'Colleen's Bride Tribe' T-shirts. Ryan, who made the reservation, was the husband of Kayla, the sister of bride-to-be Colleen. Subterfuge or not, Ramzi froze a smile.

'Just to warn you, we do our best, but in this hot weather, you may find one or two cockroaches gallivanting about,' he told them, to cover himself.

'I bet nothing like in our hotel in New York last year!' Colleen said, her allies animated in agreement.

Ramzi sighed with relief.

On the third night, the women stumbled back from a night club at three o'clock in the morning. Roused, Ramzi padded downstairs to check they'd locked up. He sighed at the sight of the valuable items left scattered round the riad. Not unusual, it showed trust, but this carelessness by guests always seemed a little insensitive to the riad's less advantaged manager Hisham and the housekeeper Latifa.

*

'Wake up, sir!'

Ramzi jolted awake as a fist hammered on his bedroom door.

'Wake up!'

Hisham? He reached for his watch—the time was six fifteen, just three hours after the Hens returned from clubbing. Still in his sleepwear, Ramzi let Hisham in.

'Why are you here so early?'

He pursed his lips, shaking his head. 'Grave news, Mr. Ramzi. There has been a robbery.'

'What!'

'Miss Colleen phoned me and I phoned Latifa. Your phone seemed dead.' Hisham opened the shutter of a window. 'They are waiting for you, Mr. Ramzi.'

Looking down into the courtyard, Ramzi saw the Hens huddled round the table. He hesitated.

'Time to bite the bullet,' Hisham said.

Taking a deep breath, Ramzi followed him downstairs.

'Good morning! Drama at dawn, I hear?' he said.

'This is no laughing matter—'

'Of course not, Irene,' Ramzi said, recognizing Kayla and Colleen's mother. 'What happened?'

'We found the door to the street wide open,' Colleen said.

'How did you discover this?'

'We put the alarm on for six.'

Three hours sleep. They had asked for breakfast only at nine. Strange! Surely married life wasn't such a bastille?

'Call the police!' Irene said.

Bang! The riad shook. With multiple cries, the group jumped.

'Was that a bomb?'

'No, just the housekeeper shutting the front door.'

'*Bonjour*!' Latifa said, breezing past them to the kitchen.

'Back to the robbery. What's been stolen?' Ramzi asked.

'A travel wallet. It had my money, credit card and a passport.'

'And your phone,' one of the brood chimed in.

'Oh yes. My phone too—'

'Stolen from where?'

'The bedroom.'

'Which bedroom?'

Four pointed left and six pointed right.

'And the door to the room was closed?' Ramzi said.

Latifa moseyed around them, a few breakfast mats in hand.

'Yes,' Kayla said.

'What make of mobile was it?' Ramzi said.

Blank stares met him in response.

'An iPhone, wasn't it? Latest model,' Colleen said.

'That's right. The latest model.'

The apparatchiks nodded approval. In the spirit of the moment, Latifa nodded too—though her English was limited to basic courtesies.

'What I need—' Colleen prompted.

'Oh yes. What I need is a crime reference number for the insurance,' Kayla said.

'What you need is a passport. You're leaving tomorrow.'

'Oh, I expect that should be fine. They put my details on the computer and stamped the passport on the way in.'

'It won't be fine. Immigration will want see something before they let you leave. At best, you'll need an emergency travel document from the consulate in Marrakech.'

Ramzi retreated to the office, certain he had locked the door the previous night. Even if a thief had broken in, the traditional Moroccan doors with the inset keyhole entrances to the bedrooms would be bolted on the inside, and anyone trying to gain entry would wake the dead. And for all the thief knew, two karate black belts could be ready to pounce as he entered—why take the risk? A quick glance showed the big-ticket items still in full view around the riad, exactly as the night before. He had a sneaking suspicion the travel wallet and passport were lost outside the riad and they wanted to hold him responsible. As for the phone—

He called the *Brigade touristique*.

'This happens all the time, sir. Tourists declaring things stolen so they can claim insurance. It is always towards the end of their trip when they have overspent. Bring them along anyway.'

Next, despite the early hour, he dialled the British Consulate in Marrakech, finding the call patched through to a helpful official with the Embassy in Rabat. Ramzi returned to the courtyard. The whir of juicer came from the kitchen as he broke the news.

'The Consulate in Marrakech is closed until Monday. The only way to get an Emergency Travel Document by tomorrow is to go to the Embassy in Rabat. They will phone me back with details.'

'Where's Rabat? In Spain?'

'Morocco's capital. About 220 kilometres away.'

'Do we need to? It's our last day!'

'Yeah. We got that spa booked.'

'How else are you going to get on the flight? Unless your passport turned up?'

Kayla hesitated.

'Alright. How do we get there?'

'I can arrange a *grand taxi*. It is quite usual here.'

'And you are coming with us?'

'Err…I don't think that is necessary,' Ramzi said.

'We could be kidnapped or have our throats cut!' Irene said.

'I expect you're paying too,' Colleen said.

Behind them, Hisham's eyes opened like saucers and he shook his head frantically.

'I expect so, yes,' Ramzi said. Hisham dropped onto a chair, head in his hands.

The conclave adjourned, Latifa appeared with a white cup and saucer.

'Coffee, Mr. Ramzi?'

'Thank you, Latifa. I need it.'

'Hicham says it's your favourite.' With a knowing look, she added, 'From the hills—'

Was it Ethiopian Yigarcheffe? He rallied, but only for a split second.

The colour resembled weak tea.

Seeing Latifa across the courtyard, he sneaked to the kitchen. Tipping the liquid into the sink, he spotted a bottle on the counter.

The same amber. From the hills—the Scottish Highlands. A single malt whisky.

'Latifa!'

*

An hour later, Ramzi, Kayla and her mother Irene stood at the desk in the Medina's police commissariat.

'If you want a document it will be easier to say the passport is lost rather than stolen,' the officer told them in English. 'How much money was in the travel wallet?'

'Two hundred pounds, and some Moroccan money. Just give me the document and the crime identification number,' Kayla said.

'I apologise, but that can only be issued from the brigade in the administrative quartier where you are staying.'

'That's bloody ridiculous,' Irene spluttered.

'Pigs,' Kayla said as they stepped into the sun.

Waving his arms, Ramzi tried to hail a taxi. On her mother's phone, Kayla phoned through to sister Colleen. A shouting match ensued.

'No, I can't say it was stolen. Check the policy. What's the max I can claim?'

By the time they arrived at the local police station, inflation had pushed the theft up to eight hundred pounds sterling.

Ramzi's phone jingled. He smiled as he took the call. 'That was the Embassy in Rabat. They can have the Emergency Travel Document today.'

'The Embassy! I can't go to the Embassy without doing my hair.'

'There's no time for that, Mum. At least you have your makeup on.'

Despite the antiperspirant, Ramzi felt sweat trickle from under his arms. He dialled Hisham. They would need water. Sidestepping a cat, stiff but alive with flies, he crossed to a small *hanout* across the road to buy bottled water.

Minutes later, a *grand taxi* squealed to a halt on the melting tarmac. The driver waved: it was Madcap Kasim. Ramzi went pale. Kayla and Irene scrambled in. Kasim crunched the gears, and they were off.

'What was that?'

'I think we ran over a plastic bottle,' Ramzi said, glad the dead cat had escaped their notice.

What a journey. The AC kaput, scalding air filled the cab as they drove a full tilt to Rabat. Kayla and Irene's squeals accompanied Kasim as he tailgated trucks, weaved through traffic, overtook on the soft shoulder, steered with his knees as he tapped a message on his phone and, just south of Casablanca, reversed down the motorway after missing a turning. At one stage Kayla's grip on the grab-handle pulled it off the door. At intervals, Irene crossed herself, sobbing, despite Ramzi's attempts to commiserate. Meantime, Ramzi provided discreet prods as Kasim's eyelids drooped and his head nodded forward towards the steering wheel.

Rabat—finally. His face sticky with dust, Ramzi's polo shirt stuck to his back as they stood in front of the Embassy.

'That's far enough for you,' Irene said to him.

'Yes. This is British territory now,' Kayla added.

Ramzi said nothing.

Irene's tousled hair and melted makeup had transformed her. He watched as a smiling clown swaggered through the entrance with her daughter.

Sighing, he turned. Kasim leant on his cab, smoking a roll-up.

'Aren't you going in with them? I thought you were British?'

'I am,' Ramzi said, tugging his passport out of a pocket, then changed subject. 'You look tired?'

'My apartment is like an oven. I barely slept a wink, what with the family moaning and groaning. It's so much cooler here.'

'I expect because we're on the Atlantic.'

A sweet, earthy smell wafted from the roll-up, nothing like tobacco. For goodness' sake!

'I'll wait by the entrance,' Ramzi said. 'In case there's a problem.'

The Emergency Travel Document secured, the relief was tempered by the fact the return journey would be partly at night—and only one headlight worked. As a precaution, Ramzi kept conversation flowing until Kasim revealed he was developing myopia and planned a visit to an optician.

Falling silent, Ramzi, switched all attention to the road ahead. From the back,

Irene grumbled about her future son-in-law not being good enough for Colleen.

As Marrakech materialised, Ramzi thanked God, and also Kasim. At the small gateway in the medina wall nearest to Riad Waqi, the taxi braked abruptly.

'I've got whiplash!' Irene cried, rubbing her neck.

'Shall we ask Kasim to turn back and take you to the hospital?' Ramzi said.

'Oh, no, sweet Jesus, no. I'm fine now.'

Ramzi opened his wallet to pay.

'We want a receipt,' Kayla said.

'I paid, so why did you want a receipt?'

'For the insurance.'

Hands on hips they stared at him.

Obligingly, Kasim opened the glove compartment, and scribbled something on a page torn from a notebook.

'What's this?'

'The receipt—'

Kayla screwed it up and threw it on the ground.

'The nerve!' Irene said, as they marched off.

'They're all the same, Mum. The sooner we're back in civilisation the better.'

Receiving a hero's return, Irene and Kayla's tale promised to rival any storyteller on Marrakech's Djemma El Fna. Amid the sneers and laughter, corks popped. Ignored, Ramzi stumbled up the stairs to his room, untied his white All Stars, and too tired to peel off his clothes to shower, fell onto the bed.

*

A hammering on the door woke him—this was becoming a habit.

'Hisham?'

'They won't pay Mr. Ramzi.'

'What?'

Retying the All Stars, he heard the muezzin call the dawn prayer. Downstairs, he looked at the luggage strewn around the courtyard. Judging by the packages wrapped in paper and string, there had been a rug-buying spree in the souks.

'Where are the guests?' Ramzi asked.

'Behind you,' Hisham said.

'I can't see them.'

'Behind you!'

The keyhole door of the salon opened, and the Hens filed out.

'I hear you want to settle your bill?' Ramzi began.

'Oh no, we don't.'

'Oh yes, you do.'

'Oh no, we don't.'

'Oh yes, you do.'

The stock phrases reminded Ramzi of the Christmas pantomimes he loved as a child in Scotland, at Glasgow's King's Theatre, and in later life, once in Pasadena, during his year at Caltech, the California Institute of Technology. Now he starred in one in Morocco.

'You have been bloody unhelpful from the start. We demand compensation,' came a yell from stage left.

'Shame!' someone shouted, pointing at him.

Empty bottles clanked in the kitchen. Latifa? Why was she here so early? He had a brainwave.

'I'll forget the surcharge on the credit card.'

'Oh, no you won't Mr. Ramzi,' Hisham said. 'That's four per cent'

'Oh, yes I will.'

'Anyway, the machine doesn't accept it.'

'Oh, yes it will.'

'Oh, no it won't.'

'Oh—'

'They're right Mr. Ramzi. It's a debit card.'

'One of your friend's cards will do.'

'No one else has a card.'

'Oh my God! We'll miss the flight!' Irene said, glancing at her watch and running to her case.

'Quite frankly, I find the fact that none of you have a valid credit card hard to believe.'

'We can call the Tourist Police to resolve the matter,' Hisham said.

'I'm telling you, we're going to miss the flight!'

'Shut up Mum!'

Folding her arms, Colleen fixed Ramzi with a death stare. 'Are you threatening me, mister?' If my fiancé were here now you'd be mincemeat in minutes.'

'No, I'm not.'

'Oh yes, you are!'

'Oh no, I'm not!'

'Look, I'll get the everyone's share, and transfer it to you when we get back to England,' Kayla said.

Colleen threw her arms round her. 'You're the best sister ever!'

Hugs over, she spun round to face Ramzi.

'Well? End of matter. Okay? Come on, babes.'

'But Miss Colleen—' Hisham began.

'Get lost!'

As the front door slammed shut the kitchen door flung open—just like Newton's third law on action and reaction, Ramzi mused, as a physicist. Except for an extra variable: it propelled a hefty fairy waving a wand into the courtyard.

Blinking, he saw Latifa with a feather duster, dancing towards the salon to clear the breakfast. The sun already dried his throat. Fetching a glass of water, Ramzi escaped to the office to type his bank details to send to Kayla.

'Mr. Ramzi?'

'Hold on a second, Hisham. Right, ready. By the way, did they give you any tips?'

'No Mr. Ramzi. That's why Latifa came to help with the early breakfast. Someone has to break her the news.'

'You're the manager—'

'But—'

'Look, both of you head off as soon as you can. We don't have guests for another two days.'

'I thought I could take you to the aqua park to cool down. We can go on a toboggan together!'

Fingers frozen over the keyboard, Ramzi manufactured a smile. Despite the heat, he could think of nothing worse. He swivelled round in the chair. 'That's kind of you to offer, but I heard it's expensive to get in.'

'I'll take it out of the petty cash,' Hisham said.

'Of course,' Ramzi said, startled. Normally, he saw Hisham as the model of thrift.

Blaming the heat, Ramzi recalled the fresher temperature in Rabat. To save his sanity, he decided to flee westwards to Essaouira and its ocean air the following morning. A couple of months back, a guest stayed there for two nights. What was the name of the riad? Riad Saffron? No, Safsaf. Riad Safsaf.

'Hisham, what does *safsaf* mean?'

'It's a tree Mr. Ramzi. The branches, they are very long and fall to the ground.'

'This?' Ramzi said pointing to the screen.

'Yes. What is it in English?'

'A weeping willow.'

'A crying tree—'

A phone call secured the last room. On the way to the water park, Ramzi bought a SupraTours bus ticket for the three-hour journey next day.

Now, lying back in bed at Riad Safsaf, Ramzi couldn't decide if the screeching of the gulls reminded him of the Hen Party, his trip to Rabat with Kasim, or the water ride on the famous Flying Toboggan with Hisham.

THREE

The hot water in the shower ran cold. Put out, Ramzi dressed, his mind absorbed by the affair of the *jidwel.* Who had delivered it and why? Was it just a warning or something more sinister?

Although the rooms at Riad Safsaf all gave to a central courtyard like his own riad in Marrakech, it had no trees or plants, rose to three floors not two, and a dissimilar decoration. Cement tiles in Art Deco geometries covered the floor setting off the French colonial furniture—brass bed, metal lampshades, slightly battered wooden side tables, a chair under a small desk. On the veneer lay the Police Registration Card. Finding a pen, he bent over to fill out his name, date and place of birth, passport details and addresses. Picking up his phone by a saucer with an empty petit four paper case, he thought how he'd liked the complimentary medjoul date stuffed with almond paste the night before. A nice touch—he would throw this budget-breaking bombshell at Hisham.

On the landing, he collided with a man in a baseball cap. Recognizing Youssef, the riad's manager, he handed over the card.

'You are British, sir?'

'Yes. By the way, there was no hot water in my room. You'd better call the plumber as soon as possible—'

At the look of surprise Ramzi caught himself; he was a guest at Riad Safsaf, not the owner. Switching subject, he asked about the flyer in his room advertising the three-day programme for an event called *hillula*.

'Yes sir. Every year the Jewish pilgrims come to Essaouira from all over the world to perform the *hillula,* to venerate the *tzaddik* of Haim Pinto.'

'*Tzaddik*?'

'A holy man, a rabbi in this case. Born in 1748, sir. The *hillula* has hours of feasting and dancing and singing and praying, so the *shekinah,* the presence of God, returns to the site of the rabbi's grave and you can ask for anything you want. Some Israelis and Americans arrived yesterday to stay with us for the celebrations; last year we had pilgrims from South Africa and Argentina.'

Ramzi nodded. 'I read that once a large Jewish community lived in the town, around forty per cent of the population, but now only a few are left.'

'Did you like the painting in your room?'

'The painting?' Thrown by the quick switch of topic, Ramzi couldn't recall it, but ad-libbed. 'Oh, that painting. Talented. Who is the artist?'

'I am the artist, sir! A lot of guests have bought my paintings.'

'I'm not surprised.'

'They are very lucky that I work here and they can talk to me. One of them said I was better than Mister L.S Lowry from England and another compared my work to *Monsieur* Henri Rousseau. They were very cultured sir. One day my paintings will also be in Paris and New York.'

'From what you say, I agree. Or even in Glasgow.'

'Thank you. It is good to talk to someone distinguished like you. Breakfast is up on the roof. Would you like coffee or tea?'

Distinguished? Ramzi made a metal note to check for grey hairs later. How strange Youssef cut his comment on Essaouira's Jewish history. Was the subject taboo, but if so—why?

Sharp sunlight and spirited breezes assaulted him on the roof terrace. Ahead, two women stood, mesmerized by some vista. One took photographs. Then, as if late for an appointment, they spun round, hurrying to the stairs.

Identical twins! Intrigued, he crossed to where they'd stood. Puzzled, he found any potential panorama blocked by the walls of neighbouring riads, encircling the lower-level terrace next door. Looking over, he watched an old fellow reeling a hose. Alongside a line of potted plants, a cat lay on a lounger, its fur lilac in the sunlight. Shuffling across, the man smiled as he bent down to tickle it.

Disappointed, Ramzi did a circuit of the Riad Safsaf's terrace, finding a ruined building on one side, high walls on the two other sides, and glimpses of the sea between. A wooden ladder lay horizontally against a parapet. Then, without thinking, he zeroed in on another elderly man, finishing breakfast.

'Good morning,' Ramzi said. 'Did you find your room comfortable.'

'Yes, thank you. Do you work here?'

Swiftly dropping his hotelier repartee, Ramzi shook his head. 'No. I'm on vacation. Did you head here for the *hillula*?'

'Right first time. Why not take a seat?'

'Thanks, just for a minute. Where are you from?'

'Israel, but I was born here, in Essaouira, or Mogador as it was called then. My parents emigrated. Being back here is a like reunion, a chance to honour my dead parents and ancestors. How can I face my grandparents in the next life if I ignore them in this one?'

Youssef arrived, bearing a circular brass tray piled-high with a breakfast.

'Good morning Mr. Spielman.' He set out crockery, an omelette, croissants, bread, butter, jams and coffee. Evidently, the trade winds had blasted etiquette out to sea as Youssef still wore his baseball cap serving at table.

'*Bon appétit!*'

'Here is my Police Registration Card,' Spielman said, pulling it from the pocket of his Hawaiian shirt.

Youssef thanked him, but as he went, he turned.

'Sir, excuse me, but I notice your name is Isaac *Knafo* Spielman?'

'Yes, it is. When I left Moga—I mean Essaouira, my surname was just plain Knafo. It comes from the Berber *akhnif* meaning cape or *burnous*, and so clearly, Sephardic in origin. Sad to say when our family arrived in Israel there was a lot of arrogance, snobbery and even claims of racial superiority from the Ashkenazi Jews against the Sephardic community from North Africa. When I was eighteen I changed my surname to sound more European and became Isaac Spielman instead.'

'Why Spielman?'

'My father played the lute, so I took the name after him. It means *player.*'

'I see sir. Thank you. Excuse me, I must attend to the other breakfasts.'

'I had no idea.' Ramzi said as Youssef left.

'Well, we arrived in the Promised Land only to have our heads shaved, be sprayed with pesticide and put in transit tent cities called *ma'abarot* near the Lebanese border. And those tents! They collapsed in the winter storms, the dirt floors turned to mud, and people and their belongings were soaked. The squalor was terrible.

'I kept thinking—how could my parents take us from such a beautiful town to live in a tent?

'To add insult to injury, we were bad-mouthed as "the dregs of the mellahs" or as "monkeys" or as "backward" and even as "garbage". In fact, the entire Moroccan and North African Jewish community were seen as psychologically unstable, and as immoral, heavy drinkers, physically ugly and even lacking the motivation to be fit and good fighters for Israel.'

'Pretty shocking stereotypes—I—' Ramzi began.

'But there's more to come. On top of this, we were expected to work in agriculture, but many had trades—tailors, metalworkers, carpenters—or professions—such as teachers, engineers or lawyers. If we said no, we were considered uncooperative, and lazy, and untrustworthy. There was an official apology to all this, thank goodness, but forty years later. Now we see the children and children's children of Jews born in Morocco are Government ministers.'

Youssef reappeared, bearing another brass tray, but stood captivated as Spielman went on.

'I helped prove these attitudes wrong. I fought in Sinai, and was awarded the Medal of Valour. Afterwards I made my way into the building trade and commerce. In those days construction was as distinguished as a job in agriculture. It fitted the ethos of Zionism and the 'New Jew' in Israel who was not afraid of physical labour, unlike their contemporaries in the diaspora. The minimum salary in Israel for a builder was more than a banker. I quickly became a project manager, and set up my own company employing ten people. Now I employ over three hundred. Of course, things have changed, and most workers these days are from Turkey, Bulgaria, and China.'

'Congratulations, that's quite a success story—' Ramzi said.

'Sure. Look how far I've come—from the Mellah in Mogador to a penthouse in Tel Aviv in Neve Tzedek, which is very exclusive.

I drive a Mercedes and have a Porsche for fun. I've appeared on television and there was an article about both myself and the company in *Globes*. I took my elder son and the family to Australia for a holiday last summer. He is in government and the other son works in America. I flew him and his wife Abigail over from New York at my expense and they can't even be bothered to join me for breakfast. Yes, Yitzak has always been a disappointment, unlike Levi, his brother. As for Abigail, she is bad news. Look, poor Youssef has been standing here with your breakfast whilst I jabber on about my life. I'll leave you in peace.' Pushing back his chair, he stood up.

'I enjoyed hearing about your good fortune, sir. Have a good day,' Youssef said.

Thanking him, Spielman walked away.

Youssef laid an adjacent table. Ramzi cast a critical eye over the breakfast: the selection of breads, omelette, jams—no honey, no yoghurt—but the coffee, a high-quality Arabica, made up for that. Stunned by Spielman's story, he felt a degree of empathy, as with a Scottish-Moroccan parentage, he had also experienced prejudice in various forms throughout his life.

From where he sat Ramzi glimpsed the sea between adjacent buildings. A seagull landed on the edge of the table. Close up, its size made him uneasy, as did a red spot looking like fresh blood on the yellow bill. Shooting forward, it snatched the butter and flew off. Ramzi's heart skipped a beat. Then another beat—his phone jingled.

'Hisham!'

'How are you?'

'I am well, thank you.'

'And how is—'

'This is no time for formalities! Have you seen the email?'

'No. What email?'

'The Hen Party are refusing to pay! Kayla says that Colleen has only one Hen Party and we wrecked it.'

Privately, Ramzi suspected more Hen Parties would be held for Colleen in her lifetime.

'And then they said, if we make trouble they will contact Travel Advisor and write a bad review.'

'Thank you Hisham.'

'You're welcome.'

Strange. He'd believed Kayla's promise to pay. His thoughts scattered as the victim of the *jidwel* stepped onto the terrace, pushing on sunglasses, her mass of dark hair tamed into a ponytail. Ramzi half-rose from his chair.

'Good morning! I apologise for disturbing you last night,' she said.

'Not at all. I can imagine the shock. Are you here for the *hillula*?'

'Yes, and to settle another matter. Then I am flying to Paris to give a paper at the Sorbonne.'

'Oh? What is your field?'

'Mesoscopic physics.'

'A subclass of condensed matter physics, if I recall. You seem shocked?'

'Disappointed. I rather enjoy people looking blank when I tell them.'

Ramzi gave a light laugh. 'Where are you based?'

'The Weizmann Institute of Science.'

'In Israel? The Institute is world famous. Before I took a sabbatical, I was a physicist too. String theory.' Although these days, Ramzi thought, the only theory that troubled him were the general principles of how he always ended up tied in knots at Riad Waqi.

'Have I said something to upset you?'

'No, not at all.' Ramzi plastered on a smile.

'And you? Are you here for the *hillula*?'

'No, I'm escaping Marrakech. It's far too hot, even for me. I have a guest house there. Are you looking forward to the festivities?'

'Yes and no. To be honest, it's been party-time since I boarded the plane. Half the pilgrims joining the *hillula* spent the flight jigging and singing in the aisles, and at

Marrakech airport, well! They turned the immigration queue into a conga line—even the security police joined in. I'm no killjoy, but I felt relieved that I was doing the journey, well over two hours, in the taxi laid on for us by Riad Safsaf, and not on the special *hillula* coach. At first, that is—but it turned out to be hateful in a different way—'

Youssef appeared, balancing another circular brass tray. 'Your breakfast *Madame*.'

Putting Ester's distress down to a taxi driver like Madcap Kasim, Ramzi gave a sympathetic nod, before heading down the winding stairwell. At the top landing, he hesitated, spotting Spielman with a young couple below.

'Sorry *Abba*. We slept in. It must be the sea air.'

Spielman glared at his son, closed the door, and without a word strolled towards the staircase. Ramzi quickly climbed a little way back up, concealing himself, until the front door banged.

'To be honest Abigail, I wish I hadn't let you persuade me to come.'

'Yitzak, you know your father is a bully. You know it. I know it. Everyone knows it. Frankly, the world would be a happier place without him. But we're here, and it is an opportunity.'

Seeing them approach the stairs, Ramzi continued down.

'Thank you,' they said, as he pressed against the wall to let the couple pass.

Lounging across his bed, as Ramzi restarted his laptop, he checked the painting on the wall by Youssef, the epitome of modesty. Setting the laptop aside, he walked across for a closer inspection. An ordeal of fish, lizards and strange-looking people, its child-like simplicity represented the Naïve Art popular with tourists. Creative, but not to his taste. He ran his finger over the top. No dust. He nodded approval.

Back to the matter at hand, he logged in to scan the offending email from Kayla, and did a little research. Research! Out of the blue, it hit him that one reason why he had left his university department was a nagging suspicion his prime research field had crashed into a theoretical cul-de-sac. For a moment, he sat in a cloud of gloom until, overcome with curiosity, he googled Israel's Weizmann Institute of Science, Faculty of Physics. There she was: Ester Fraeknel. Publications in high impact journals. Impressive.

Ploughing on, Ramzi decided to write to the Fraud Department of Travel Advisor warning them of the threat. He recalled Kayla's husband Ryan had paid the deposit for the booking through PayPal—and lo and behold!

Below 'money received' he found an address located in Bristol, in the South West of England. Straight to Google Maps, he fixed on a small terraced house in a cookie cutter development. How did all that square with the designer handbags and expensive clothes paraded by the Hens during their trip? Still, this was no time for musing but for research—and Ramzi began benchmarking Debt Collection Agencies in London.

The gulls cawed and the noise echoed through the courtyard like laughter.

FOUR

Out in the old town, Ramzi wandered between whitewashed buildings dappled by the sea air and the elements and, unlike the riads in Marrakech's historic Medina, their windows facing to the street. The doors were mainly blue, the others green or yellow, most framed with stone surrounds, arched or squared, some set with tiles, many crowned with six-sided rosettes and even Stars of David—or were they representing the six-sided star on the former Moroccan flag? Often too, the doors stood cheek-by-jowl. Did they open to shops, or stairs or corridors? And where were the numbers? As a scientist, it all lacked logic.

A boy thrust a shoebox towards him, sniggering as Ramzi flinched. Quivering inside were chirping chicks, varyingly dyed purple, pink, blue or green. Psychedelia: hadn't the electric guitar legend Jimi Hendrix been in Essaouira at some point in the 1960s?

Ramzi walked onto the *Sqala*, its bronze canons pointing from the ramparts out to the crashing sea. Along its length, tourists posed for photographs. By contrast to their shorts, polos and T-shirts, several men, some with side-locks, wore dark trousers, white buttoned shirts, black fedoras or the *kippah* skullcap. Walking on, he stopped by a cannon, gazing down at the Portuguese shield, dated 1780.

'Hello Ramzi.'

He jumped. 'Dr Rashida! What a shock!'

'Am I that scary? By the way, perhaps it's time to drop the title? Rashida is fine.'

'You're right. I don't mean about being scary, or maybe just a bit, well you know what I'm saying—so what are you doing here?'

'Such diplomacy! Isn't a doctor allowed a little holiday from her patients?'

'Of course. Who are you with?'

'Are you suggesting a woman cannot spend time alone or without a chaperone? You are old fashioned.'

'I mean—I didn't mean—'

'Essaouira is a perfect place to windsurf—'

'Windsurf! I—Shall we go for a coffee?'

'How about dinner? There's a nice restaurant *La Petite Perle*. Eight o'clock.'

Ramzi watched her leave, unable to continue on. Turning her head, she smiled and gave a small wave. Dr Rashida—Rashida—always left him with a sense of disorientation, like the lanes on this walk. Retracing his steps—in case she thought he was stalking her—he headed back down and into an unknown alleyway, stopping to puzzle over another sandstone carving above a doorway, five snakes in a line crowning two snakes wrapped around a rosette.

'Hello again!'

Turning, he recognised the man holding a small bottle of Sidi Ali mineral water.

'*Monsieur* Spielman!'

'Isaac is fine. Are you enjoying Essaouira?'

'Yes, quite a change from Marrakech and cooler. Are you sightseeing or stepping down memory lane?'

'You could say a bit of both.'

'I was just looking at this stone carving.'

Spielman followed his gaze, then pointed above the door. 'Those snakes on top are protection from the evil eye and the two below symbolize the couple living in the house, but they also guard the five-petal flower. Meaning, I suppose they will be good Muslims.'

'The petals representing the five pillars of Islam. I see.'

Spielman walked a little ahead and waved a finger in the air. 'And this carved flower with four petals showed the house belonged to Christians.'

'Well that's a few mysteries solved—'

'Good. Let's walk together. We're almost on the edge of the Mellah.'

'The old Jewish quarter—?'

'You'll join me, won't you my brother?'

'Err—well, I—'

'Nothing to be jumpy about. Look, just along here was the synagogue of Rabbi Isaq Smmara right next to the old Talmudic School. I went there as a child.' He pointed to two doors, with arched stone surrounds.

'Our classes ran from eight until sunset, and on the Sabbath, from eleven until four o'clock. We learnt Hebrew, we recited the Talmud together with its teachings, and read the Arabic translation of books of saints.'

Ramzi followed him through a short tunnel. Spielman stopped to explain that in the building above them was another synagogue, Slat l'Qaha. Beyond, was a lopsided quarter: on one side, crumbling facades; on the other, hard earth stretching to the town walls, broken by concrete benches—even a stray dog looked perplexed at the asymmetry of it all.

'Believe it not, this was the main street in the Mellah. You cannot imagine how full of life it was. There were houses and shops too on the left, but as you see, there're all gone. Razed to the ground! It's criminal this happened.' Spielman brushed some tears from his eyes and, taking a few paces, surveyed the urban wilderness. 'My grandfather used to have his tailor shop right here. Orson Welles shot part of his film, Shakespeare's *Othello* in Mogador—I mean here in Essaouira. The crew and actors all arrived, but the costumes ordered in Italy had yet to be started. It was the Jewish tailors who saved him. My grandfather sewed tunics from jute sacks usually used for almonds, and made armour out of sardine cans. There was a scene in a Turkish bath—actually they used the fish market—and we had to run to find all the incense we could to imitate steam.' Spielman laughed. 'He was clever, that guy!'

'Did your family sell their house?'

'Yes, but not at market value. It was difficult; everyone was selling to go to Israel. You can see how the buildings have fallen into disrepair. The population drained away like blood from a body, and the Mellah died.' He threw open his arms at the dereliction before them. 'Just look at it—a disfigured corpse.'

'The synagogue of Haim Pinto,' Ramzi said, reading a sign. 'Isn't that the saint?'

'The *tzaddik*. The reason for the *hillula*—yes. A pity it says to telephone to visit.'

'Actually, there are some visitors coming out now.'

Confirming it was open, they entered and climbed the stairs. At the top was a painting of Rabbi Haim Pinto, with a full white beard and orthodox black brimmed hat. Elsewhere, in a sepia photograph, a shawl covered his head. Beyond was a large room, with a cross beam ceiling of slender tree trunks. Two benches lined opposite walls. Between these ran blue panels, centred with a curtain, the navy velvet embroidered in gold with Hebrew and a crown.

'That's the *anet*, the holy ark, on the eastern wall facing Jerusalem—it symbolises God's presence in the synagogue. Above, that lantern is the eternal light, the light of the Temple. Somewhere behind will be the Torah scrolls—'

'Would you like to see?' a voice said.

They turned. A woman in a *hijab* and glasses stood in the corner. Pulling back the curtain, she opened a panel. Inside, the scrolls, the height of a child, were wrapped in cream cloth mantels, cushioned against a blue quilted wall.

'What's this platform for?' Ramzi asked.

'The *bimah*? It's where the Torah is read and the Rabbi gives the services. It's in the centre of the chamber so everyone in the congregation can hear it. Up there is the balcony where the women sat. And this decorated cloth on the table is so the Torah doesn't rest on natural wood. Let's go. All this blue painted timber, I don't like it, it's not how it was.'

Spielman pulled notes—American dollars, Ramzi noticed—from his wallet as a donation. Back outside they walked on, passing a collapsed dwelling, with a menorah, the seven candles lit, painted onto one of the patchwork of rooms.

Spielman veered into an alley with an open sewer.

'How times have changed. On the Sabbath, this used to smell of *skhina*.'

'Hot? The same word as Arabic?'

'Right. It was a spicy stew, with bulgar wheat and eggs. The eggs were cooked and peeled afterwards so they took the flavour of the stew. It tasted of history and survival. The families took it here to the *farran*, the communal wood fire.' He pointed into a vacant building, 'That died too.'

He sighed as they branched into an impasse. In front of them a wall fountain, green with algae, dripped tears.

'I used to collect water there for my mother.'

'You had no plumbing back then?'

'No. Let's go.'

Doubling back, they saw an elderly man limp heavily into the shadows.

'*Oy vey!*' The colour drained from Spielman's face.

'Are you okay?'

'It's all too much. I shouldn't have come—'

Ramzi tended to agree. The sewerage, the collapsing buildings, the old man with a limp: the combined effect was eerie.

Returning to the wasteland, the flood of sunlight and the tang of sea in the breeze, seemed invigorating yet Spielman remained pale, tottering a few steps to a concrete bench.

'Are you alright?'

'Just a twinge in my chest. Angina. It's probably nothing, just give me two or three minutes.' From his trouser pocket, he took a black pillbox, the enamel set with a gold bee, clicked it open and picked out an orange-green capsule. Popping it in his mouth, he put his head back and washed it down with water from his bottle. 'I always worry this'll fall out my pocket,' he said, snapping the pillbox shut.

Ramzi sat beside him. A short time passed. At last Spielman spoke, as if trying to put life back into the dereliction.

'The Belisha family used to live somewhere over there, but that house has gone now, like most things. One of them emigrated to England and his grandson became high up in Government.' He stood up. 'I'm okay, now. Let me show you this: that bricked up arch was an old distillery for *mahia*.'

'*Mahia*? In Arabic that means *eau-de-vie*.'

'Right. It's a spirit made from figs, raisins, dates or jujube and scented with aniseed. It has quite a kick.'

Reaching a final bend, he glanced back. 'Look what I've done—'

After a moment, Ramzi said, 'Well, thank you for sharing your story with me—'

'I doubt Yitzak is interested, but I could be dead tomorrow. Now at least it won't get lost in the tapestry of life. Someone knows.' Reaching Bab Doukkala, a trio of gateways in the town wall, they paused. 'I'm going on to the cemetery. Thank you, my brother.'

'Not at all,' Ramzi said, but abstracted, Spielman disappeared through an archway.

Emigrant, war hero, construction tycoon. Yes—look at what he had done!

Ambling back towards the port, Ramzi bought a copy of the Moroccan daily *Le Matin*. For the first time, he noticed the headline of Gregorian, Islamic *Hijiri* and Berber *Amizagh* dates side-by-side with the Hebrew calendar. Reaching the *Café de France*, he found a table looking towards the harbour and ordered a coffee.

Belisha. It sounded familiar. He checked Wikipedia on his phone. Messoud Belisha, a merchant from Essaouira had emigrated in the late nineteenth century to Britain. His grandson Leslie, later the Lord Hore Belisha, was at St John's College in Oxford, where he was president of the Oxford Union, fought in the First World War and later qualified as a Barrister. Entering politics, he became Minister of Transport, introducing the Road Transport Act, which brought in the driving test, as well as the amber beacons on black and white poles at pedestrian crossings, named after him by the public.

Of course! *Belisha Beacons.*

They conjured a moment of nostalgia, but Ramzi read on. Appointed Secretary of State for War by Chamberlain, Belisha's position became untenable due to disputes with the King and Army high command as well as with the public supporters of Oswald Mosley of The British Union of Fascists, who condemned him as a 'Jewish warmonger.' Lord Gort, commander of British Expeditionary Forces in France, disliked him to the extent that his private secretary wrote in his diary, 'the ultimate fact is that they could never get on—you couldn't expect two such utterly different people to do so—a great gentleman and an obscure, shallow-brained, charlatan, political Jew-boy.' Undeterred, Chamberlain considered Belisha for the post of Minister of Information but the Foreign Office raised concerns about the appointment of a Jewish politician in this position given the undercurrent of antisemitism amongst portions of the public in England—

Irritated, Ramzi put down from his mobile, gazing into space. What had Belisha felt? Anger, sadness or embarrassment? Had he lived in a subconscious state of vigilance, as the target of discrimination—a recipe for emotional stress, in an already stressful position? For the second time that morning Ramzi felt empathy. Stereotyped by his looks, Ramzi had spent much of his life trying to ignore micro-aggressions of snubs, slights and misguided comments. He thought back to just three days ago, to the reaction of his guest Irene when, British passport in his pocket, he offered to escort them into the Embassy in Rabat. At least, since arriving in Morocco the feelings of tension and anxiety he suffered disappeared, as he no longer needed to navigate the moral outrages about an imagined mind-set.

Smacking a ten dirhams coin on the table Ramzi folded the newspaper and looped back to Riad Safsaf.

FIVE

Closing the front door, he heard a woman's voice: 'I am not paying you anything. Over my dead body! You can stay tonight, but tomorrow clear out before I'm tempted to kill you.'

As Ester strode off, Ramzi thought this dramatic but splendid. Perhaps he needed a course on assertiveness training to deal with his own guests in Marrakech? After his paternal grandfather died in Scotland, at the funeral parlour of the Chapel of Rest, he had been captivated by one such training diploma framed on the wall, next to the licence from the British Institute of Embalmers.

'Guests!' she said. 'Are you *Monsieur* Ramzi? Did you complain about the hot water this morning?'

'I'm not sure,' he said, wincing. 'Maybe.'

'Whether it was you or not, the hot water is back in business. I apologise.'

'No need to apologise.' Ramzi's face brightened. 'I own a riad in Marrakech, and know the headaches. Perhaps we can recommend each other?'

'Why not? I'm Poppy by the way.'

Ramzi opened his wallet, sliding out a few crumply business cards, the garish ink smudging he did so. He handed them all across.

'Wow! So many!'

'Don't worry, my manager ordered ten thousand.'

Poppy laughed. Ramzi thought she might have laughed louder if she knew it was true. She handed across her card, sleek, silky, crisp and classy on premium paper. Or it was, until he saw the ink stain from his thumb—

To deflect attention, he said, 'Tell me! Do any of your bedroom doors have locks? We often have guests complaining.' The ghosts of clients of the past, including the Hen Party, loomed in his mind. 'The difficulty being, that like here, many doors are heritage pieces, and too traditional to spoil.'

'I agree, but it was the one thing that drove me mad. Anyhow, I confess I just gave in and whoopee! Next week we'll have quite a clever carpenter to arrange locks for all the doors but,' she lowered her voice, 'between ourselves, to make our life easier, he'll make sure one key fits all! Meantime, wander at will!' Laughing, she turned. 'Youssef! I wondered where you were.'

'If I can do my job *Madame* Poppy? That's why the guests like me. Would you like some mint tea, sir? I am making some for the two guests over there.'

'Thank you, Youssef.'

'The key was my idea,' he smiled.

Sighing, Poppy disappeared into the office. Across the courtyard, stone arches opened to a sitting room. Inside, the twin sisters perched on a Louis XVI-style sofa, another legacy from the colonial epoch.

'Hello. I'm Ramzi.'

'Are you something to do with the riad?'

Ramzi reddened. 'No. I'm a guest. I saw you this morning, but you rushed off.'

They glanced at each other.

'Are you here for the *hillula*?'

'No, I'm not, are you?'

'Yes!' they said in unison.

'I'm Rachel.'

'I'm Rebecca.'

'Where are you from?'

'We're based in Jerusalem. We flew in last week to research an article on the Jewish Community in Casablanca,' Rachel said.

'What's left of it,' Rebecca added.

'I write.'

'I photograph.'

'I saw you taking pictures on the terrace this morning.'

They fell silent. 'A cat!' Rebecca said.

'I saw it. Such a beautiful colour,' Ramzi said.

Rachel jumped in. 'And here in Essaouira, we're doing an article on the *hillula* and the *tzaddik*, Rabbi Haim Pinto.'

'Do you have a family link to Morocco?'

'No. Our grandmother was Lithuanian and our grandfather Russian. They emigrated to Israel after the war.'

'Tell me about Rabbi Haim Pinto. I visited the Synagogue this morning. Why is he so special?'

'His miracles. In the nineteenth century, he was only twenty when he became head of the Rabbanic court in Essaouira and remained so for seventy years.'

'Was that the miracle?'

Youssef interrupted with the mint tea. Into three small glasses he poured the amber liquid at height from the curved spout, creating a foam on the surface. Ramzi made a mental note to mention his nails needed a scrub, but recalled this was not his riad. Could he never switch off?

'Shall we go on?' Rebecca asked.

'Of course. I was a bit distracted.'

'People said that when a stranger came to see Rabbi Haim Pinto he knew everything about him. Also, it was known that his disciples heard him answer their questions before they asked them.'

'And tell about the Eliyahu Hanavi!'

'The Prophet Elijah. Well, when the Rabbi rose every night to study the Torah his assistant would prepare a cup of coffee. One night the assistant awoke a bit late. Running to make the coffee he heard two voices. The next day the Rabbi asked why he'd made two cups. "I thought I'd prepare a second cup for your guest." To which he replied, "Happy are you, as you heard the voice of the Prophet Elijah but repeat the secret to no one."'

The twins both picked up their glass of tea and solemnly sipped it.

'Wow!' Ramzi said. 'I wasn't expecting that—'

'There's more!' Rachel said. 'Once, in the middle of the night, Rabbi Maklouf came on a matter of great importance to the community in Essaouira. Entering the room of Rabbi Haim Pinto, he saw his face illuminated, and beside him someone who resembled an angel. Afraid he ran home. The next day Rabbi Haim Pinto said to him, "Happy are you, as you had the honour of seeing the Prophet Elijah."

'In fact, Rabbi Makouf lived till a 110 and recorded this in his prayer book.'

'No way,' Ramzi said.

'And during the bombardment of the port in 1844, almost 600 Frenchmen invaded. As Rabbi Haim Pinto left the synagogue, a soldier drew his sword to kill him but his hand became paralyzed and the weapon fell to the ground.'

'Heavens! Well he was certainly a legend in his own time.'

'Not only then, but now,' Rebecca agreed. 'There's the story of the vendor of merguez sausages and chips in a kiosk in Casablanca. One day, the oil ignited and his clothes caught fire. As he screamed, in front of him appeared the image of the Rabbi. The man shouted "By the virtue of Rabbi Haim Pinto, save me from death". Suddenly a hidden door, which had been covered with plaster, opened behind him and he ran out. He had third degree burns and was in hospital for several months, but was saved.'

'Quite amazing—'

'And the girl!' Rachel said.

'Oh yes. A girl became mad after her mother died. The family tried everything, but all their efforts failed. Finally, they drove to Essaouira and tied her to the tomb of Rabbi Haim Pinto. In minutes her manner changed and she recovered her sanity and went on to lead a normal life.'

Despite his own experiences of strange events in Morocco, Ramzi was sure a psychiatrist would raise an eyebrow on hearing this. However, he said nothing, suspecting that any negative comments might be blasphemous.

'You almost forgot this one!' Rachel said to her twin. 'Recently, there was a blind teenager, who was frustrated he could neither study nor pray. He asked his family to take him here to the Rabbi's tomb. In tears, he asked, by the virtue of the saint, to recover his sight. The following morning when he woke up, he could see.'

'Where is the Rabbi's grave?' Ramzi asked.

'Beside the European cemetery north of the town, outside the wall. His shrine is in the old cemetery, and the new one is across the road, with a reception hall, where the *hillula* is celebrated.'

'Talking of which, is that the time? We had better get ready for the *hillula*.'

They hurtled upstairs to their room.

SIX

'Youssef! Is *La Petite Perle* nearby?'

'There's a map in the salon, *Monsieur* Ramzi. I'm a very busy man, as you can see.'

Ouch! Still, a quick look at a street plan showed it as just around the corner. Ramzi wound his way from the square. The restaurant was in an old depository with stone vaulting, lined with red, green and gold tent wall covers and brocade banquettes. Candles lit the low tables. Ramzi promised himself not to mention how romantic it looked as he waited outside for Rashida.

'*Bonsoir*!'

'*Bonsoir* Ramzi! I see it's already busy.'

The waiter led them into the depths of the room, and they sat opposite each other.

'What are you having?'

'The fish soup and calamari tagine,' Rashida said, putting aside her menu.

'Likewise, the soup, but I'll go for the octopus tagine. They don't serve wine here, by the looks of it, but water is fine.'

Order taken, a small silence ensued.

'Isn't this romantic?' Ramzi said. Oh God! 'What I mean is, how was the windsurfing?'

Rashida laughed.

'It's hard to describe. It helps me escape from everything. Of course, it is challenging but I feel at one with nature. Time stands still. It makes me feel so happy and strong.'

'Much like I felt when I went rock climbing—'

'How is your holiday here?'

'I think I should have rented a small apartment. At Riad Safsaf, I feel like a cross between a detective and a hotel inspector.'

'Oh?'

Ramzi started explaining about Youssef, the quality of the breakfast, the imperious riad owner, the nocturnal interlude of Ester and the *jidwel*, Isaac Spielman, his story and the tour through the Mellah, his son and daughter-in-law, and the twins and their account of Rabbi Haim Pinto's miracles.

'The soup is excellent, but yours is getting cold.'

Ramzi picked up his spoon. 'On top of this, I don't really understand why the Jewish

Community left Morocco after centuries? Aaron, a friend of mine, explained about the *Aliyah,* the longing to make the ascent towards Jerusalem by moving to the Land of Israel. But the sudden rush to go?'

'The Jewish Community were always bound by restrictions of some sort or another, and victims of terrible, murderous incidents, but through the ages, the Sultans, for the most part, protected them. At times they were ministers, administrators, negotiators and ambassadors to the Royal Court. If I recall my history, when the Sultan signed the Treaty of Fes with France, establishing the Protectorate in 1912, the Sultan's troops mutinied but couldn't attack the protected European quarter in Fes, so they attacked the Mellah.'

'The Bloody Days of Fes.'

'Apart from dozens of deaths, hundreds of Jewish homes and shops were destroyed. After this, I think the Jewish Community began to view Muslims with suspicion, and felt the Sultan couldn't protect them.'

'I read the riot was the reason the French—Governor General Lyautey— moved the capital to Rabat.'

'It had been a capital centuries before. The city was on the coast and had less religious and political significance. Anyhow, the French colonists soon dominated the Protectorate's economy at the expense of the Jewish economy. This in turn triggered emigration. A few thousand left Fes for Jerusalem in the 1920s, but a forfeit of 1,000 francs per person, quite a fortune in those days, was seen as a deliberate policy to prevent a mass exodus.

'Then came the war. In the 1940s the Nazi-controlled Vichy Government administered discriminatory decrees. All Jews living in the French quarters in the cities were ordered to return to the Mellah. Of course, this led to overcrowding and health issues, like child mortality and trachoma. On top of this, Jewish children were expelled from French-run schools. Many Jews lost jobs in administration, and were forbidden to trade with the French. There were quotas for doctors and lawyers. Can you believe Jewish doctors were not allowed to treat Christians or Muslims?'

Rashida paused, taking a drink of *Oulmès* water.

'That's terrible,' Ramzi said, pouring more sparkling water into her glass.

'That was not all. The Vichy regime demanded that the Jews wear a yellow star, like in Nazi occupied countries in Europe at the time, and there was talk of mass deportations to concentration camps—but King Mohammed V refused. He declared there were no Jewish subjects, nor Muslim subjects, there were only Moroccan subjects, who were all under his protection.

'Of course, the Vichy administration was soon ousted by the Americans. Although saved by the King from the Holocaust, there was an anti-Semitic backlash after the declaration of the establishment of the state of Israel in 1947. The next year there were mob riots around Oujda.'

'Oujda? Near the Algerian border?'

'Yes. The Muslim population were irritated by the Jews using it as a hub to leave for Israel via Algeria. They were seen as combatants for Israel. Allegedly, the French stayed in their barracks to avoid the conflict. More people died, more were injured and more had property destroyed. Zionist organisations took advantage of the situation, playing on the fear and vulnerability of the Jewish Community, and it triggered a stream of emigration. The French tried to block it, but in the end, relented and set up a transit camp near Casablanca.'

Soup bowls whisked away, the tagines arrived. Lifting the conical lids, clouds of steam escaped as the waiter left them. Heady aromas of paprika, ginger and cumin rose from the pink and green stew of baby octopus, onion and olives.

'It looks and smells delicious,' Ramzi said, tearing the flatbread.

'I love the turmeric and fresh coriander they've added. Now, where was I? Okay—when Morocco became independent in 1956, the right-wing government severed ties with Israel, and passed decrees banning immigration and passports. The Israeli secret service Mossad helped get around this with fake passports and bribes to corrupt officials. They distributed leaflets arguing that the Jewish Community no longer had a stake in Morocco. Emigration was relaxed and there were rumours that a payment was made by Israel for each Moroccan Jew that emigrated. In twenty years 250,000 thousand people had left. The Arab-Jewish tensions with the Six Day War in 1967 were the *coup de grâce*.'

'Two or three million Muslim Moroccans emigrated during those thirty odd years too, for political reasons. My mother included,' Ramzi said.

'True. Anyhow, after Mohammed VI took the throne, many things changed. The King affirmed Hebrew as part of the national identity, said he welcomed any Jew who wanted to return. As you may know, his senior advisor is a Jew. In fact, a representative of the King always makes an official visit to Essaouira during the *hillula*. He established full diplomatic relations with Israel, and now, from the last year of primary school, the history and culture of the Jewish Community is on the curriculum.'

'Now your tagine is getting cold.'

Rashida dipped some bread into the spicy tomato sauce.

'Thank you for the tutorial,' Ramzi said.

'I look forward to marking your homework. Really, this tastes so fresh—'

Ramzi planned to pay, but Rashida trumped him.

'Well you must let me pay for the next meal.'

Rashida smiled. 'Tomorrow night? That's if no one has been murdered at the riad in the meantime?'

SEVEN

Meandering back from the restaurant, Ramzi replayed the conversation at dinner, but as he turned into the covered alleyway to the riad, he sensed someone following him. About to put the key into the lock, the man stopped.

'I didn't mean to alarm you. I'm staying here too. Oren,' he said, extending a hand.

Ramzi shook it, introducing himself. Seeing Oren's small black skullcap, he said, 'I expect you're here for the *hillula*?'

'How did you guess?' He gave a broad smile.

'I thought tonight you'd be celebrating with the other visitors?'

'I was, but left early. I'm going to have a whisky on the roof terrace. Care to join me?'

'Thank you. I'll just get a jumper.'

'Good idea.'

Minutes later they sat with backs against the breeze listening to the sea break against the rocks.

Looking at the label, Ramzi swirled the amber liquid in his glass.

'*M&H*. I don't know this whisky.'

'It's a Single Malt. *Milk and Honey*. Made in Tel Aviv.'

'It's very good,' Ramzi said, a little surprised. 'I imagine the heat and humidity must be a bit challenging in Tel Aviv when compared to the glens of Scotland.'

They laughed, then sat for a moment staring into the night. Ramzi broke the silence.

'It's a long way to come to drink Israeli whisky—'

'I came to ask the *tzaddik* Haim Pinto for advice or a message.'

'Ah. Yes, I heard he can be helpful.'

'Not so far, unfortunately,' he said. They heard the front door bang. 'That's someone else back. Are you here on holiday?'

'Yes, but I have my own guest house in Marrakech. The temperatures last week almost melted the tarmac.'

'We flew in from Madrid. It hit me as soon as I stepped off the plane. But at least a heat without Tel Aviv's humidity. I was glad the riad sent a taxi to take us here directly.'

'We?'

'Ester. We happened to be on the same flight.'

'What's your line of business?'

'Construction.'

'Then you must know Isaac Spielman? He is also in the building trade.'

Oren drained his glass. 'It slipped my mind; he was in the taxi too. Anyway, it's late. I think I'll turn in.' He screwed the cap back on the bottle and said goodnight.

Warmed by the whisky, Ramzi lingered on for a time, aware that Oren tensed at the mention of Isaac Spielman, and bizarrely, clean forgot he rode from the airport in the same taxi, a journey of two-hours plus. Maybe a genuine mistake, or was he camouflaging some connection between them? Certainly not friendship considering the abrupt way he cut the conversation. About to pull on his jumper, Ramzi thought the better of it, preferring to head to bed.

On the saucer on the nightstand, the stuffed medjoul date tasted of honey, a little like the Israeli whisky, but without the hint of oak. Teeth cleaned, he climbed between the slightly damp sheets. They reminded him of seaside holidays visiting his paternal grandparents in North Berwick. Such carefree days, playing in the sand with a bucket and spade on one of the bays, swimming in the Firth of Forth—a quick shiver recalling that—

eating a '99' cone of vanilla ice cream speared with a stick of flaky chocolate…

A cry broke his sleep, plus the sound of someone retching. Was he in a dream where he'd gobbled too many '99' ice creams? No—it was real.

Ramzi scrambled out of bed, pulling on trousers and a shirt, the floor tiles cool beneath his bare feet. He knocked on the door of the next room.

'Are you okay?'

He heard a whispering.

'I'm coming in,' Ramzi said, opening the door.

Doubled over, Spielman looked terrible, not helped by the pineapple-print satin pyjamas. Staggering about, he clutched his stomach. A stench of diarrhoea wafted from the bathroom.

'*Monsieur* Spielman?'

He fell to his knees, and hands on floor, vomited. Ramzi crouched beside him. Spielman looked up, tears on his cheeks, repeating something in Hebrew.

'I don't understand.' Ramzi said.

'Returning, returning,' he whispered in English.

Ramzi turned him on his side, to prevent choking. Standing, he nearly upset the night stand. Grabbing the lamp and date dish, he steadied it.

'What's happened? I'm Abigail, his daughter-in-law.'

'By the looks of it he's had bad diarrhoea and you can see he's been vomiting. I think a bit delirious: he keeps saying he's returning. We know that.'

'Oh, it's nothing—he's had too much food and *mahia* at the *hillula* this evening. He always was a bit of a glutton.'

Abigail flushed the toilet and brought a towel to wipe Spielman's mouth.

'I'll get a doctor.'

'No, that's really not necessary.'

'All the same—'

Back in his room, he phoned Rashida.

'Ramzi. It's five-thirty in the morning. Are you mad? Or are you passing the time before heading to the mosque?'

'I've spent more time at church.'

'I forgot, you're a crusader.'

'In a manner of speaking. We have a problem with a guest at my riad.'

'There's always problems with guests at your riad.'

'No, here in Essaouira. He's ill and looks near to collapse. Vomiting and diarrhoea.'

'I'll meet you outside the *Café de France* in ten minutes.'

Spielman lay on the floor, unable to move. As Abigail mopped up patches of sick with a towel, her husband appeared in shorts and flip-flops.

'*Abba*? Good God!'

'You father's had too much to eat and drink Yitzak,' Abigail said, hurling the towel into the shower tray. 'Or it's some sort of food poisoning.'

Yitzak knelt by him. 'What's happened to his eyes? The pupils are dilated. Let's move him to the bed.'

'Leave him,' Ramzi said. 'I've phoned for a doctor. Keep him on his side in case he chokes. I'll be back in five minutes.'

Ramzi arrived at Place Moulay Hassan as the muezzin called the dawn prayer. Hovering in front of the *Café de France*, he shivered a little. What a holiday!

'Good morning Ramzi.'

'You've come equipped.'

'I always have my doctor's bag with me. Lead the way.'

Now Ester stood at the doorway of Spielman's room. She gave way as Ramzi and Rashida arrived.

'He's been having convulsions. His fingers and toes are blue,' Yitzak said. 'And now he stopped moving.'

'The floor's cold,' Abigail said.

Down beside the patient, Rashida opened her bag, pulling on latex gloves. 'The blue is cynosis—lack of blood oxygenation.'

Lifting his eyelids, she flicked on a pen torch. 'Mydriasis. He's in a coma.' Turning him gently, she unbuttoned his top, putting a stethoscope to his chest. 'His heart has slowed. He needs support. Call an ambulance, now!'

On the landing Ramzi dialled one-four-one and gave the address and directions. Back in the room a tearful Yitzak leant against the wall.

'His heart stopped—'

Rashiha tilted Spielman's head back, checked his mouth for obstructions, before listening for a breath. Interlocking her hands, one on top of the other, she began rapid compressions in the centre of Spielman's chest, followed by two rescue breaths.

Without a word, they watched as she repeated the process. Finally, Rashida shook her head, and stood up.

'I'm sorry. There was nothing more I could do. What's the time—?'

Ramzi looked at his phone. '5.48'

'Are you sure, are you positive?' Yitzak asked Rashida.

'I can only reply with my condolences.'

'*Blessed are You, Lord, our God, King of the Universe, the Judge of Truth…*' Yitzak began, kneeling beside his father.

'I'm positive it was something he ate, or just over indulgence,' Abigail repeated.

'Forgive me, *Madame*,' Rashida said. 'It may well have been food-poisoning or as you suggest, over indulgence, but legally we are required to contact the police as your father-in-law died outside his home or a hospital. I am going to close the room until they or the paramedics arrive.'

On the landing Ester said, 'I think he could have been poisoned and that poison was meant for me.'

'Yoo-hoo!'

Hearing the heavenly duet, they all looked up. The twin sisters leant over the railing of the second-floor landing.

'You woke me.'

'And me.'

'Can we come to the pyjama party too?'

'What fun!'

'*Monsieur* Spielman is dead,' Rashida said.

Three loud knocks made them jump.

'The paramedics,' Ramzi said.

A bedroom door opened, and Oren emerged wearing a baseball cap back-to-front and in running gear.

'Has something happened? I thought I was the early bird.'

'*Monsieur* Spielman is dead.'

'Are you serious?'

'Yes, I'm a doctor.'

‘So, Spielman is dead,’ Oren said, and burst out laughing.

‘That’s insulting,’ Abigail said.

‘Nervous reaction. I really am sorry. What a terrible event.’

The paramedics charged onto the landing carrying a kit bag and flexible stretcher.

In the next instant, Oren dodged through the crowd towards the stairs.

Yitzak wiped away tears, and sighed. ‘It’s over! I’d better phone Jerusalem to break the news to Levi.’

Abigail hugged him. ‘Let’s get changed,’ she smiled, ‘It’s too early to call the boys in America.’

Ramzi watched them leave. Was that a smirk on Yitzak’s face?

EIGHT

The guests gathered in the salon off the courtyard. Coffee, mint tea, and a bowl of croissants covered the coffee table.

'I hope this is okay, though I imagine no-one is very hungry.' Poppy said. 'Saturday is Youssef's day off, so call if you need anything. What a thing to happen.'

'The staff having Saturdays off?' Ester said.

'You know perfectly well I mean *Monsieur* Spielman's death. It's a terrible thing.'

'Well, at a certain age, food and drink can be lethal,' Abigail said. 'Isaac was such a kind, honest and wonderful man. We will miss him.'

Ramzi's astonishment was masked by Ester coughing and gasping for air. 'Sorry, I swallowed my coffee the wrong way.'

'Excuse me,' Poppy said, 'I've one or two things to attend to.'

Ramzi asked, 'I wonder when the symptoms appeared?'

'He was feeling ill at end of the *hillula*.'

'Was he, Abigail? He looked well, though a bit tipsy when Rachel and I walked back with him together,' Rebecca said.

At the doorway, Rashida interrupted them to present Inspector Hassani.

'The room must remain closed for now. This is very unfortunate. His Royal Highness the King's representative arrives today. All of you must remain here at Riad Safsaf until you have been interviewed. I would also like your passports.'

'I think we will need an autopsy,' Rashida said.

'You can't do an autopsy,' Oren said quickly.

'Why not?' Inspector Hassani said.

'According to Jewish tradition, the soul is in a state of anxiety and anguish until it's buried in the ground. The more it's cut up and explored the more agitated it becomes.'

'Yes, the body belongs to no one but the Almighty. The issue is seen by the Talmud as theft,' Rebecca said.

'And disgracing the human body. Desecration of a dead body is prohibited,' Rachel added.

'You're right,' Abigail said. 'Our duty to the One Above is never to insult the Creator.

Man was created in the divine image. Our body is the Almighty's and we are mere caretakers. An autopsy will disfigure the body.'

'Also, don't forget the Torah's commandment *halanat ha'met*—it prohibits the body being left overnight before the burial,' Oren added.

'Without wishing to sound callous, it is usual in a case like this to examine the gastric contents, a hundred grams of the brain, a hundred of the liver, fifty of the kidney and vitreous humour from the eye,' Rashida said. 'If you allow it, I am sure we can guarantee all organs and body parts and fluids will be interred with the body.'

'I'm not sure my brother Levi in Jerusalem will agree,' Yitzak said.

'But surely if it helps identify a killer?'

'We do not know if there was a killer, it was only Ester who said this.'

'Yes, but if he was murdered, the autopsy could discover that the dead person—my father—was suffering from a terminal condition. That would spare the murderer anyway,' Yitzak said.

'So, now he could actually save a life,' Ester said, with a note of contempt.

All looked at each other. Ramzi's head spun.

'Cremation is not allowed so that is one less worry.'

'But buried where? Here?' Yitzak said.

'I need to seek advice on this matter,' Inspector Hassani said.

'Fortunately, this weekend there are quite a few Rabbis in Essaouira,' Ramzi smiled, a quip met by a stony silence.

'I meant from the Ministry.'

'This is a nightmare. I need to phone my brother—again,' Yitzak said.

'Well that's done,' Poppy said, joining them.

'What's done?' Abigail asked.

'I've just put the towels and soiled linen from *Monsieur* Spielman's room on a hot wash in the machine, and mopped down the floor with bleach.'

Inspector Hassani broke the silence. 'Why did you do that?'

'I keep a clean riad. All the vomit and diarrhoea, it's not hygenic.'

'That was evidence, *Madame*,' the Inspector said.

'Oh, you're right. I didn't think,' Poppy said.

'Obviously not. That may well complicate the investigation. I could have you arrested for obstruction of justice.'

'You could, but you're not—'

Inspector Hassani looked at her. After a small silence he said, 'If you would like to accompany me, Dr Rashida.'

Ramzi followed them.

'Where are you going, sir?'

'I was joining Rashida—Dr Rashida.'

'I said everybody must remain at the riad.'

'I'm a suspect?'

'Exactly.'

Downcast, Ramzi returned to his room. There was a text on his phone from Rashida.

I always thought you seemed shifty.

Shifty? He examined himself in the mirror. After a shave, stepping into the shower, he was reminded of Abigail, also cleaning things up. Was she neat by nature, or trying to hide something? After all she continued to insist that either food poisoning or overindulgence caused Spielman's death. As Shakespeare wrote, *The lady doth protest too much, methinks*—'

His phone jingled. Grabbing a towel, he wrapped it around him, and picked up the mobile.

'Hello Mr. Ramzi! Are you relaxing by the sea?'

'It's a bit early. How is the riad?'

'There's a scary email. Miss Colleen and her tribe won't like it.'

The towel slipped off Ramzi's waist.

'Thank you Hisham.'

'You're welcome.'

Stark naked he checked the mail on his phone.

The debt collector had forwarded a *Letter before Action*, which read:

> *Payment has been properly requested. You ignored these requests. Your creditor has with reluctance had to instruct us. This issue is clear. We are to collect payment forthwith.*
>
> *WE REQUIRE YOU TO SETTLE THE DEBT NOW.*

Ramzi's heart palpitated and his palms moistened. Hold on—he was the creditor! Still, at full tilt, he dressed and darted from the room as if threatened by a baseball bat.

Downstairs, he only found Rebecca, carrying breakfast dishes towards the kitchen.

'I thought I'd give Poppy a hand.'

'Good idea,' Ramzi said, collecting the remaining items. 'Is she destroying more evidence from a possible crime scene?'

'You think it was murder?'

'It's a suspicion, according to Dr Rashida. By the way, what happens at the *hillula* dinner?' he asked, sliding the jams and butter into the fridge.

'Beforehand there's ritual slaughter of animals to share the meat with as many pilgrims as possible. There's also an auction of tea glasses and candles. All the money goes to the upkeep of the cemetery and the tomb.

'Dinner is served with *mahia*—well, non-alcoholic drinks too—and people become rather ecstatic. There is dancing, singing and chanting, mostly of the Psalms. Everyone looks for signs of the *tzaddik* in our midst or making an appearance in the form of an animal in the cemetery or close to the shrine. This is because many pilgrims believe a *tzaddik* can manifest themselves in the form of animals.'

'I see,' Ramzi said.

'The *tzaddik* can also speak through someone at the *hillula*.'

'Good gracious! Like a medium?'

'Kind of. We heard that last year a stranger walked up to one of the pilgrims and, out of the blue, she told him his wife had given birth to a daughter. "Impossible!" he exclaimed. "She is not due for at least two weeks, that's why I came alone to get a blessing." Well, a few minutes later his phone rang—with the news that his wife had gone into labour early and he was now the father of a baby girl.'

'Can I help?' Abigail stood at the doorway, in a long, floaty dress.

'No, we're just about finished.'

'Did anything strange happen at the *hillula* last night?' Ramzi asked.

'Nothing that I know regarding the *tzaddik*. On the other hand—'

'Yitzak! Did you manage to speak to Levi?'

'He wants Abba's body to be buried in Israel.'

'Why not bury your father here? Most of his ancestors are buried in the Jewish Cemetery. He told us that he looked at the graves yesterday.'

'You know Levi. He reminded me the Torah describes how, before their deaths, both Jacob and his son Joseph asked to be buried in the Promised Land.'

'That's all very well—'

'Then he talked about the Talmud. Of course, we all know it states that being buried in the Land of Israel brings a certain measure of atonement for sins. Yet, Levi went on, one quote after another, *Anyone buried there is buried beneath the altar*, and *His land will atone for His people*.'

'Well, your father certainly has a lot to atone for!'

'Abigail!'

'To be honest, I tend to agree with your wife,' Ester said.

A policeman stood at the doorway. '*Monsieur* Ramzi, Inspector Hassani would like to interview you now about the death of Monsieur Spielman.'

Just as the conversation took an interesting twist! Reluctantly, Ramzi followed.

*

'*Monsieur* Ramzi. Please take a seat. I believe you found *Monsieur* Spielman and phoned Dr Rashida?' the Inspector began.

'Yes.'

'How did you know her? Why not call emergency services on one-four-one at once?'

'We became friends in Marrakech. I met her in Essaouira by chance. I thought Monsieur Spielman might just have some gastroenteritis or overindulgence like his daughter-in-law suggested. Dr Rashida was just a few minutes away.'

'How did the victim appear prior to the symptoms?

'Yesterday morning, he showed me round the Mellah. Or what is left of it. He seemed in good health.'

'Do you know if he ate anything during the day?'

'No, we parted. Of course, he went to the *hillula* that evening and by all accounts enjoyed the meal.'

'He didn't seem angry or unhappy?'

Ramzi hesitated at the question.

'Go on—' Inspector Hassani said.

'If anything, he seemed sad. Sad about the Mellah being so run down. Despite being successful in Israel, I think he missed Essaouira, and Morocco in general, but maybe that's an age thing. Nostalgia. I think it was stressful for him as he had a slight chest pain, angina he said, so had to sit down. And—'

'Yes?'

'Monsieur Spielman was quite exasperated with his son and his wife. He flew them over from America and planned breakfast together. They rose late—maybe the jet-lag. So, he had the morning to himself. That's how I bumped into him near the Mellah.'

'He didn't mention any of the other guests?'

'No.'

'Did anything else unusual happen?'

'Well—'

'Go on.'

'That morning there was a *jidwel* charm, pushed under a guest's door. It scared her. You see, a *jidwel*—'

'Yes, I know what a *jidwel* is. Who was the guest?'

'Ester.'

'Do you think, if there was a murder, the intended victim was *Madame* Ester?'

'She thought so.'

'Oh?'

'She thought he had died by mistake and that the poison was actually meant for her.'

'Did you find anything unusual at the crime scene?'

'No. I was more concerned with attending to the victim.'

'Or did you notice if any physical evidence was removed from the crime scene? Remains of food and drink, glasses, bottles, medicines, soiled clothing?'

'To be honest, that was the first time I had been in his room. If anything was taken I wouldn't have known. If it is of any help, I can say for certain, Abigail—his daughter-in-law was cleaning up the vomit and flushing away the diarrhoea. Plus, as we heard, Poppy admitted to having washed the towels and clothing.'

'From our conversation, Abigail, his daughter-in-law, seemed very attached to him.'

Ramzi hesitated, recalling the small drama on the landing the previous morning.

Inspector Hassani continued, 'What intrigues me is why you chose to stay at Riad Safsaf? Are you here for the *hillula*?'

'No. I own a riad in Marrakech. One of my guests stayed here and I remembered the name. I wanted to escape from the heat in the city. It was all a last-minute arrangement.'

'That I understand. Essaouira has a nice balmy temperature. That aside, you had no idea about the *hillula* or know any of the guests?'

'Absolutely not.'

'I think that is all for now.'

'Am I free to roam?'

'Just stay in town, *Monsieur* Ramzi.'

NINE

Released, Ramzi found the group had broken up, so hopes of continuing the conversation on atonement were dashed.

He phoned Rashida, arranging to rendezvous at the *Café de France.*

Fifteen minutes later he found it not only a relief to be out of the riad and in the open air, but to sit at a table on the esplanade with Rashida.

'I almost wondered if Inspector Hassani suspected me.'

'You are Scottish.'

'Meaning? Why are you so stern?' Ramzi said.

'I suspect *Monsieur* Spielman was poisoned, so I called CAPM in Rabat.'

'CAPM?'

'The Moroccan Anti-Poison Centre. I described the symptoms. They speculate it could be *atractulis gummifera.* The Glue Thistle.'

She smiled. 'Just the word thistle suggests a Scottish signature on it all...'

'What!'

'In fact, it grows in Southern Europe and North Africa. They suggested we check on a spice shop in in Souk Laghzal that they collaborate with.'

'The wool market?'

'Yes—but that's also where the spices are sold—and fish.'

'So far, nothing in Essaouira is what it seems, don't you think?'

Buffeted by wind, they cruised up the pedestrian Avenue d'Istiqlal, drifting through the tides of people in flamboyant clothes, channelled by low cliffs of white walls and sandstone arches, the drapery of kaftans, tunics and textiles splashing them with colour. Fighting the flow, Rashida sailed leeward through an archway carved with Kufic script, into a space protected by a gallery of arcades, and Ramzi followed, into a harbour of calm.

From the nearest shop, a dried eagle, a dried porcupine, a shrivelled lizard and dried gourds hung over a stand of traditional cosmetics.

'I'm looking for Mr. Othman.'

'Is it something for your couscous *Madame*? Henna for your hair or *khol* for your eyes? Or this lipstick?' He uncapped a tube and twisted up a green baton.

'Green is not my colour.'

The vendor put some on his lips. It reddened them. 'Magic, *Madame.* Or you prefer some Moroccan Viagra for your husband?'

Ramzi blushed.

'This is just a friend.'

The vendor gave a knowing look. 'Well Othman is two shops down.' He turned towards it and shouted, '*Ya* Othman!'

Like a jack-in-a-box, a young man shot up. He spread his arms over pyramids of powdered saffron, paprika, cumin, ginger, and *ras-el-hanout*, tagged as perfect for fish, chicken, lamb and vegetables.

'Welcome my friends!'

'Let's get straight to the point. I was given your name by CAPM.'

Glancing round, the smile faded. 'Quick, into the back.'

Squeezing past him into the shop, they sat on opposite benches. A framed photograph of the King, Mohammed VI dominated the room. Bottles of prismatic liquids lined the shelves. Switching on a dangling lightbulb, the vendor drew a curtain across the doorway.

'Do you have anything, how shall I put it, toxic?' Rashida said.

'The Arab poet Rumi wrote: *A snake's poison is life to the snake; it's in relation to man that it means death.*'

'Poets tell great truths,' Ramzi said.

'I can see this man is thinking of his wife.'

'Except I'm not married!'

Othman smiled benignly, and went on.

'*Tikiout* or *Euphorbia resinifera.* It goes back to the Roman Emperor Augustus. Mix it with flour and egg white to treat stings and snake bites, and it can be used to fumigate against bad spirits. However, the latex will suit your purposes: it is very dangerous. Just 0.5 gram can cause serious inflammation of the mucous membranes as well as gastroenteritis. At high doses the victim can die of asphyxiation.'

'Hmm. Not quite the effect I was looking for.'

He laughed. 'Perhaps you have venom enough ? What about *mandragora autumnalis*? Known as *Bayt el Ghoul*.'

'Home of the Djinn?' Ramzi said

'Mandrake in English. They say a demon lives in the plant root.' Othman pulled a large jar off a shelf. Inside a thick, dark brown root, branched into what looked like leg and arms of a human monster. 'Legend has it that this can kill a man if it is freshly picked. Often a dog was used to pull it out. As he did, the mandrake would shriek and the dog would die. The root is used as a narcotic, and if it is burned, the smoke helps asthma as well as hay fever. It contains alkaloids such as atropine, hyoscyamine and scopoline. They can cause dizziness, vomiting, a dry mouth, a purple face and eventually, a coma.'

'*Hot as a hare, blind as a bat, dry as a bone, red as a beet, mad as a hen*. The mnemonic for atropine poisoning.' Rashida leaned forward, and said quietly. 'What about *atractulis gummifera*?'

'*Addad*? Or the Glue Thistle—spiny leaves with a pink flower. Its white gummy tears are sweet, as tragically some children have found to their cost.'

The vendor pulled a plastic box from under the bench. Unclipping the lid revealed a dozen or so scorpions climbing over each other. Ramzi and Rashida recoiled.

'I love doing that!' Othman hooted with laughter, replacing the lid. 'No, it is this box.'

His face became solemn as he lifted out a woody root, about thirty centimetres long.

'Dried, this is a good remedy for syphilis.' He shot an impudent look at Ramzi, who protested. 'The plant is still widely used in traditional medicine for therapeutic purposes against dizziness and headaches, against bleeding during childbirth, gangrene, for haemorrhoids, skin cancer, healing or cauterizing wounds, and bleaching teeth. I've had patients use it to induce abortions. The root is very toxic and can be fatal. The fresh root is perhaps five times more lethal than the dry. Prolonged boiling—-two or three hours—can reduce its impact.'

'Sounds exactly what we are looking for,' Ramzi said.

'May I add. If your wife drinks, the poison is especially potent when combined with alcohol.'

'Like *mahia*?'

'That can be seventy percent proof if it is contraband. Your wife certainly has a strong constitution. Perhaps one drink too many makes her violent?'

'I don't have a wife,' Ramzi insisted.

Othman gave him a wink. 'No, of course not.'

'Is there an antidote?' Rashida said.

'Not that I know of.'

'Where is it from?'

'Frankly, *Madame*, I get mine from the dune forest to the east of Essaouira.'

'Well thank you.'

'Of course, you will want time to think.'

He drew back the curtain as they stood up. Showing Rashida out, he turned to Ramzi.

'Be careful my friend. Don't forget the saying: *If you want to take revenge on a man, send him a beautiful woman*.'

Outside, in the arcade, a group of tourists were inspecting the spices.

'Thank you,' Rashida said. 'The cardamom tea should sort my husband's bad breath perfectly.'

'And don't forget: chew the *miswak* twice daily.'

The sightseers scattered as Ramzi passed.

After a few moments Rashida said, 'You don't have bad breath by the way.'

'Thank goodness for that,' Ramzi said, his voice squeaky. 'What's a *miswak*?'

'A tooth cleaning stick, a bit like a pencil, from the Arak tree. Anti-bacterial and pre-toothbrush.'

'So back to business. You think the poison was the gum thistle?'

'*Atractulis gummifera*. Yes.'

They had settled in a hidden café, under a sprawling fig tree.

'Perfect to mix with *mahia*. Have you tried it?'

'That's a cocktail that's escaped me,' Ramzi said.

'I meant the *mahia.* It's made of figs, dates or aniseed, pretty strong and very sweet.'

'Perfect for my grandmother.'

'Not your wife, the violent alcoholic?' Rashida said.

'Please stop. Let's look at the opportunity. What if gum thistle was added, but by accident drunk by someone else in the group?'

'Good point. Or perhaps Spielman committed suicide?'

'Masochistic. I can't see why. Yesterday he was boasting to me about how successful he was.'

'Maybe returning after all these years tipped him over the edge?'

'Well, his mood changed on the trip down memory lane in the Mellah, that's true. But I can't imagine him becoming suicidal. Besides he invited his son and daughter-in-law to join him.'

'To say goodbye? To tidy matters up afterwards?'

'I don't think that adds up. Maybe he did have some terminal illness and—'

'Well, the autopsy will show that,' Rashida said.

'If it goes ahead.'

'In fact, Yitzak brought up the point about the discovery of a terminal illness absolving a murderer. Perhaps he knew more than he was saying.'

'Absolving himself? That might explain why he wanted it to go ahead.'

The subject of death sparked the idea of visiting the Jewish Cemetery, where the *hillula* happened the night before. They settled the bill and strolled to the northern city gate.

Ahead, two graveyards stood across from each other, both surrounded by a tall white wall.

A woman in glasses and a *hijab*, stood at the gateway of the cemetery to their right. Recognizing Ramzi from his visit to the synagogue the previous day, she invited them inside. After showing them a function hall for events, including the *hillula*, she ushered them out to the cemetery itself. Twenty or so people negotiated their way between the graves, the slabs arranged haphazardly, parallel to the sea, or perpendicular one to the other. Some visitors took photos; some bent over to make out the carvings.

'It's bigger than I thought,'Ramzi said.

'Seven hectares in total,' the custodian said, still at their side. 'The female tombs are engraved; the plain stones are the resting places of the men.'

Ramzi and Rashida picked their way between the tombs. A few names and epitaphs remained, all in Hebrew, but most were obliterated by time, only leaving traces on the women's graves of stylised figures, often crowned with flowers or isosceles triangles, the points inward to the brow. Chanting against the perimeter wall were a group of men, draped in white tallit prayer shawls.

'Can we see the shrine of Haim Pinto?'

'That is in the older cemetery. The smaller one.'

At that, custodian nodded towards a padlocked box. Above it read, in Hebrew, French and English:

CHARITY PRESERVES FROM DEATH. DONATION FOR THE MAINTENANCE OF THE CEMETERY. THANK YOU.

Folding a hundred dirham note, Ramzi pushed it into the slot.

'Thank you, sir. We also sell *mahia* at the *hillula* and have an auction of drinking glasses to help with the upkeep of the shrine and maintenance.'

She led them out. Across the road a pedlar set up a handcart of barbary figs. A blue carriage drew alongside the wall, and two men clambered out. The custodian waited whilst they paid the coachman, pushed open an entry and left. Beyond, the white gravestones were dominated by the shrine of the *tzaddik*, an octagonal building with a blue tiled roof, a queue of pilgrims waiting at its steps.

Ramzi could feel the wind and hear the sea. With little new to discover he suggested setting out back to town. Reaching the ramparts Rashida stopped at the gateway, turning to face him.

'Ramzi, I just had a thought. Maybe you ought to find out a bit more about Riad Safsaf. Its owner, for instance?' she said.

'Poppy? Was putting potential evidence in the washing machine an accident or by design?'

'That too—'

'Good thinking. You could be my sidekick?'

'As much as I'd love to be your Watson, I can't.'

'May I ask why?'

'I'm off to windsurf. After all, that's why I'm here!'

TEN

Ramzi settled back in one of the blue and white chairs of the *Café de France*.

Nearby, he recognised the elderly man from the next-door terrace, sitting with two pre-teen children, a boy and a girl. Laughing at their chitchat, the man appeared to tease them, smiling to return their adoring looks. Ramzi switched his attention to the square. There, amongst the beach bums passing in their uniform of T-shirts, beads, shorts and flip-flops, Poppy stood out in her white blouse, cropped trousers and burgundy loafers, a file of papers in her hand. What a fluke!

He leapt towards her. 'Poppy! It's been quite a morning. You must be drained! May I buy you a coffee?'

'Sure, how kind of you. Inspector Hassani gave me a hard time for "tampering with evidence". Then I had to run to an appointment at the notary.'

Ramzi pulled her out a chair.

'*Bonjour,* Émile!' she called across the tables, with a small wave. 'One of my neighbours,' she explained as she sat down, 'with his grandchildren, Jules and Lilou. He's charming—a real gentleman. French. Married late. Now he's ninety-odd. Says it's to do with the sun and sea air. He's been living here for years.' The waiter hovered beside them. Ramzi, already buzzing from the caffeine overdose that morning, opted for a bottle of sparkling *Oulmès* water.

'Shouldn't the kids be at school?'

'They're at the French School here. The *Eric Tabarly*. But today's a Saturday.'

'Of course, it is. Whereabouts in Morocco are you from?'

'I'm not, I'm from Canada.'

'Canada! What brought you here?'

'Believe it or not—Othello!'

'Othello?'

'It's a long story. I married straight out of university. My husband and I set up a software company—what a success! We were very much in love, life seemed hunky-dory, but my husband's love turned into a psychosis. He started accusing me of infidelity. He checked my cell phone and emails. He wouldn't even let me watch television in case I saw an attractive man and fell in love with him. Into the bargain, he started accusing various neighbours and friends and even an employee of having an affair with me, then hey, he started checking my financial records and put me under surveillance.'

'I see now. If I recall from school, in Shakespeare's play, Othello murders his wife Desdemona as a result of a mistaken belief that she has been unfaithful.'

'Exactly right. Nicky—Nicolas—was diagnosed with early onset Parkinson's disease. What happened was attributed to that. In the end—well he committed suicide.'

Her voice caught, and Ramzi worried she might cry. He made a play of looking for a tissue or hanker-chief in his jean's pockets.

'I am sorry.'

'Thank you. It was a difficult time. At one stage, trying to understand him and the delusional behaviour, I researched Othello's Syndrome. Up came the film *Othello* by Orson Welles, part of which he made here. There's a square named after him just outside the city walls.'

Ramzi told her about Spielman's grandfather, the tailor, and the solution to conjure up the missing costumes on a tight budget.

'I read something about that. Anyhow, I think it was a chance to get back to my roots that also prompted me to come—and to escape what had happened and another

Canadian winter. Then, when I arrived, I felt so at home here. I had some money and bought this riad. I still oversee the software company. Nowadays it's easy with the internet, and the time difference helps.'

'Your roots? But you said you were Canadian?'

'Second generation. Originally my family were from Palestine.'

Ramzi, unsure how to reply, said a diplomatic 'Oh?'

Poppy shook a sachet of sugar, tore the top and tapped some into her coffee.

'My family were from Safsaf, in Galilee. Near the Lebanese border.'

'The willow-tree. The name of your riad.'

'Exactly.'

'So—Canada. What happened?'

'Have you heard of the *Nakba*?'

'The Palestinian Catastrophe?'

'That's it. Some would call it ethnic cleansing, and others as defending the Jewish state. I know what I call it, though. *Haganah* entered the village in 1948. On October 29th—'

'*Haganah*?'

'During the British Mandate of Palestine, it was known as the Jewish Paramilitary. It then became the core of the Israeli Defence Forces, the IDF. It was part of

Operation Hiram. Before they came, they bombarded the town. Muhammad Zaghmout, the famous singer, was with a group of villagers working in the vineyard and was killed. Because of the shelling, the family couldn't bring the body back.

'The village expected, I'm not sure why, the Jewish attack to come from the east, but didn't. It came from the west. At sunrise, the village was overrun. They raised the white flag. *Haganah* rounded everyone up in the village square. Men and women were separated. Israeli sources claim that fifty-six men had their hands tied and were shot. My family says seventy men were blindfolded and murdered. They included my great-grandfather and my father's teenage brother. Four women—one fourteen years old—were raped in front of the other villagers and one bayonetted in the stomach, while eight months pregnant. Ten more men were from the Zaghmout family, another ten of the Shryadeh family. The accounts vary, but the horror was the same.

'One way or another our family and other families had been in Safsaf for generations. Now, they and the rest of the villagers were driven out, unable to collect their possessions. They fired gunshots over their heads. A few boys, including my father and several elderly men were allowed to stay to bury the bodies. My father was seven and he buried his older brother.'

Again, her voice wavered, but taking a moment to compose herself, she continued.

'The *Haganah* took our goats, sheep and mules. A few days later the troops reappeared and told the remaining villagers that if they forgot what had happened they could stay in their village. No harm would come to them, they said. Of course, no one believed them. Why would they after what they did?

'Our luck, if you call it that, was that my grandfather was away, working. He was a mechanic with the British during the Mandate. He still cannot talk about what he found when he arrived home. He joined the villagers leaving at night in small groups. Near the Lebanese border they were stopped and searched by the Jewish forces. They confiscated my grandmother's gold jewellery—part of her dowry—and the little money my grandfather had. All we have left is the key of our house, a beautiful old key, longer than my hand. There was always hope that as long as we had the key it would be possible to return.

'However, that never happened, because two days later, Galilee, once almost exclusively Palestinian was completely occupied by the Israeli army.

'Yosef Nahmani, was a senior officer in the *Haganah*. In his diary, a few days later, after listing atrocities in other villages nearby, he wrote something like, "Where did they come by such measures of cruelty, like Nazis? Is there no more humane way of expelling inhabitants…?"'

'That's a surprising analogy from an Israeli patriot. Surely, comparisons to Nazis are both inappropriate and offensive.'

'Yes, terrible though this was, we were victims and not part of the systematic extermination that happened during the Second World War.'

'And Safsaf now?'

'The first Israeli Government passed laws that prevented Arabs returning to their homes or claiming their property. Apart from a few houses, all was reduced to rubble, like most Palestine villages. It was renamed, Safed. Two years later Bulgarian Jews built a settlement on the village's land, our land, where we had farmed for hundreds of years. Kfar Hoshen they called it, and later Jews from Yemen and Tunisia also settled there.'

'And Canada? How does that fit in?'

'My family crossed the Lebanese border to be settled in a camp. My grandfather managed to get to Beirut. In 1955, Canada decided to accept a small number of refugees. They had immigration opportunities for

Palestinians too. My grandfather said there was an outcry in the Arab Press about it, claiming it was a Zionist plot, a Western conspiracy to despatch us from our ancestral lands and any emigration should be forbidden.

'Anyway, it went ahead. Fortunately, at the time, my grandfather was in his thirties—the limit was forty-five. Many people applied, were accepted, then dropped out. We were settled in Port Arthur—now it's called Thunder Bay—in Ontario on Lake Superior. As soon as he could afford a house my grandfather planted a weeping willow in the garden. Safsaf was never forgotten. And I can assure you, what happened to my family Palestine, I won't ever let happen to me.'

Absently she ripped the sugar sachet, and white crystals spilled onto the table.

'Isn't the poppy Palestine's national flower?'

She smiled sadly. 'Yes, that's right, hence my name. My grandfather had sons and I was the first girl grandchild. He always said I lit up his life like the poppies lighting up the countryside. Though, of course, they also represent remembrance—and death.'

A short silence followed. To Ramzi, it seemed strange—Safsaf became Safed. Port Arthur is Thunder Bay. And Essaouira had the Portuguese name Mogador until the 1960s. If only it were that easy for a country or its people to change their identity—

Something else occurred to him.

'Tell me, did the guests for the *hillula* book in independently or through an agency?'

'A mixture. Why?'

'Industrial espionage: I'm just thinking that I could get some business next year for anyone wanting to stay in Marrakech before and after. Sorry have I upset you?'

'No, it's this wasp! Oh, thank goodness, it's gone.' She stood up. 'I must go now,' she said, and put three, ten dirham coins on the table, alongside spilled sugar and the sachet torn to shreds.

ELEVEN

After the luxury of a siesta at Riad Safsaf, Ramzi freshened up with a splash of cologne, deciding on a stroll before meeting Rashida for dinner. As he left the room, Rachel and Rebecca called down over the railing from the upper landing.

'Did you survive the interrogation?' Ramzi asked, looking skyward.

'The Inspector was a sweetheart. But what a day! We were just going to have a pre-dinner drink. Care to join us?'

Ramzi hesitated, but thought it a good opportunity to talk to them.

'Thank you,' he said.

'Well, get a glass from your room and pop on up!'

Tumbler in hand, Ramzi found their door open.

'Come in! Do you know *Tubi 60*? We brought a couple of bottles from Israel.'

She handed him the bottle with a cloudy yellow liquid. The label, black and white, had a bird on it with a lemon branch in its beak.

'No, this is new to me. What's in it?'

'No one really knows. In Jerusalem, it keeps us buzzing on a night out.'

'I put fizzy water with mine. I find it a bit bitter otherwise,' Rachel said.

'I prefer it neat. What about you?' Rebecca chimed in.

'I'll try it straight first.'

Rachel took the *Tubi 60* and poured him a shot.

He sat facing them on one of the single brass beds, high off the floor. They sat opposite, swinging their legs in unison as they talked.

'What do you think?' Rebecca asked.

'About Spielman's death?'

'That too. But I was talking of the *Tubi*—?'

'Not bad. It tastes a bit like the Italian liquor *limoncello*, with herbs.'

They giggled.

'Did you go to the *hillula* with Spielman last night?' Ramzi asked.

'I took some pictures of it. I can show you later.'

'We were sitting near Spielman. It wasn't a great swan song.'

'Meaning?'

'He seemed to be drinking quite a bit and started boasting about his war record in Sinai,' Rachel began.

'During the Six-Day War?'

'Yes, back in 1967. From what he told us, under enemy fire, he pulled three men to safety behind an abandoned Egyptian tank. The people around us started applauding and he stood up to take a bow.'

'It was a pretty harrowing story. Ester started crying and left the table.'

'In fact, I think she disappeared altogether,' Rebecca said.

'I think you're right, come to think of it.'

'As if that wasn't enough, he started bragging about a new contract to build Israeli settlements in East Jerusalem.'

'Isn't that in occupied Palestinian territory?' Ramzi said.

'Whatever. Anyhow, Abigail looked shocked. Yitzak tried to get him to sit down.'

'Then he called Yitzak a pathetic coward and Abigail a traitor to Israel. Or words to that effect.'

'What happened then?'

'Yitzak and Abigail smiled politely, but left at some stage. I didn't see them again until he became ill a few hours later.'

'And Oren—' Rebecca said.

'Oren?'

'We saw him having an intense conversation with Spielman at the back of the hall. Then he disappeared too. Earlier, just after one of the songs.'

'What was the song?'

Rachel became serious. 'It went something like this, in English.

The saint is here! The saint has come!
To bless and cure, grant wishes and hearts' desires!
To pardon past wrongs,
To think of present needs,
Follow the good path, and
Share passing wealth
To deserve merit.'

'Actually, I met Oren when I came back from dinner.' Ramzi said. 'Spielman returned to the riad alone, then?'

'No! He came back with us.'

'I misunderstood. I reckoned when you said "together" earlier this morning, it meant with Yitzak and Abigail.'

'Not at all.'

'How was he on the walk back?'

'A bit drunk. He ranted a bit. First, he said he was going to report Oren's company to *Kav LaOved* and the Coalition against Construction Accidents—'

'Who are they?'

'Israeli non-profit organisations to protect rights of disadvantaged workers. He told us he knew of a death of a migrant worker that fell from a scaffolding and Oren covered it up. He threatened to tip off the media,' Rebecca said.

'A bit ironic. The number of construction workers killed on sites is two and a half times that in Europe. The average site is visited by an inspector, every three years,' Rachel said.

'You said, ironic? How?'

'I have heard of several accidents over the years—some also fatal—linked to Spielman's own company.'

'There's safety in success,' Rebecca said with a small laugh.

'After telling us that, he rambled on about how he valued life, and not gambled with it like his son,' Rachel said.

'Meaning Yitzak?'

'Yes. It seems he is a *refusenik*.'

'*Refusenik*?'

'Originally it meant anyone denied exit from the Soviet Union to emigrate to Israel. Now it's used for someone who refuses to serve in the Israeli Defence Force. There is mandatory conscription in Israel, both men and women. Apparently, at the time, Yitzak told his father that if he did military service he would be contributing to the occupation. His father was furious. As he'd been a military hero, he felt it dishonoured not only his family, but also Israel.'

'I can imagine. Were you conscripted?' Ramzi said.

'Yes. Though women serve a shorter time.'

'We could have found a reason to avoid it, but we thought why not serve our country?'

'It was useful. We learned *Krav Maga* for example.'

'What's that?'

'Hand-to-hand combat. Let me show you,' Rebecca said, jumping off the bed and crossing the room. 'Come on, over here. Don't be a coward. I won't hurt you. Now, make a swinging motion like you have a knife and want to attack me.'

Half-heartedly, Ramzi obeyed. In a flash, a whirlwind of limbs left him flat on the floor.

The sisters laughed.

'Our rooms have different floor tiles,' Ramzi said when he opened his eyes. Picking himself up, he brushed down his clothes, and bounded to his drink.

'Any news on whether there'll be an autopsy?'

'Not that I know of.'

'Do you think it was food poisoning? Or over indulgence, like Abigail said? He had quite a belly!'

'Or just plain poisoning!'

The twins exchanged looks.

'Why do you think that?' Ramzi said. His phone rang in response. Apologising he took the call.

'Hello?'

'Did I get the venue wrong Ramzi? You're missing a romantic sunset.'

He looked at his watch.

'I'm en route.' He drained his glass. 'Sorry I'm late for a dinner date. Thanks for the *Tubi 60* and demo. Maybe we can talk again tomorrow?'

'Yes please!' the twins said in unison as Ramzi raced from the room.

TWELVE

'Hi again, Poppy. Is the *Taros* restaurant nearby?'

'Yes. Go right at the end of the lane, beyond the *Café de France*. It's on the corner of the square.'

Ramzi shot off. Outside, the late evening blushed the white façades edging Place Moulay Hassan. At the corner, he climbed the stairs to a roof terrace, criss-crossed with coloured lights over lantern-lit tables. Rashida sat gazing over the darkening port with its square citadel and beyond to the smudges of islands. Smiling, he almost skipped across to see her. She nodded to a bottle of rosé wine.

'*P'tit Mogador*. I thought it would be appropriate. In fact, when I phoned you, the colour almost matched the sky.' The waiter poured. Ramzi gave a big grin, both at the wine and the waiter's manicured hands.

'Are you OK? You're not stoned, are you?'

'Why do you think that?

'You look slightly euphoric. Excited, with sparkling eyes and a goofy smile. Either you found the murderer or maybe seeing me has that effect?'

'No, not you, guests at the riad—the twin sisters—Rebecca wanted me to attack her, and threw me to ground. They gave me this Israeli drink, *Tubi 60*. No, it was the other way around. They gave me the *Tubi 60* then I attacked her. I mean, well, of course, seeing you—'

Rashida laughed. 'Well that's a relief. So, you failed to figure out who is the murderer—if there was one?'

'That just about sums it up. However, just as you called, Rebecca made a throwaway comment about Spielman being poisoned. That's the second person who mentioned that.'

'Apart from me—'

'Yes, I am beginning to lose count.'

'Well, first Ester, now Rebecca. That's interesting. I wonder why?'

'I hope to find out tomorrow. Unless they are the poisoners, and it was to throw me off the scent. Their mood changed.'

'Poisoners do try to take charge of the investigation…'

'I didn't know that.'

'His daughter-in-law Abigail kept insisting that the cause of death was because he went overboard at the *hillula* dinner.'

'Well, it seems it wasn't just with the food and *mahia*—'

Rashida listened as Ramzi recounted Spielman's farewell performance at the meal.

'Four people, Abigail, Yitzak, Ester and Oren left the *hillula* early, but at different times. That gives each an opportunity, if not a clear motive.'

'According to the twins, Ester seemed overcome at Spielman's heroism.'

'But, don't you recall, after Spielman's death she said she wasn't surprised if he was poisoned by accident and she'd been the intended victim?'

'If that was the case, she could be in danger. Still, it might be all stage-managed, so I would still keep her as a suspect. Rachel and Rebecca too, as they agreed with her? They had no real alibi after walking him back to Riad Safsaf. If they settled him in his room, anything could have happened there.'

'Such as administering a poison.'

'Exactly.'

'Mission accomplished by the way. I talked to Poppy, the owner of the riad. It seems her family were refugees from the *Nakba*. She was born in Canada. Riad Safsaf is named after the village the family left.'

'The tree that weeps.'

'She's the second generation, but quite bitter. Even though they seem to have been successful in Canada.'

'I imagine the family were scarred by it. However, bitter enough to murder an Israeli citizen? Especially as Spielman emigrated from Morocco? It sounds a little farfetched. And why stop at one?'

'He was born in Essaouira. Was booking into Riad Safsaf more than a coincidence?'

'I doubt it. He probably had an inkling that the name was familiar.'

'True. He said they were settled in camps near the Lebanese border, and Safsaf is in that general area. Spielman's family emigrated after Poppy's family became refugees, and he was a child at the time. I can't see any motive there, except political. After all, there are five other Israelis in the riad for the *hillula*. Why him?'

'Good point.'

'Apparently, she was married. Her husband became jealous of her, convinced she was being unfaithful. He ended up committing suicide.'

'Othello syndrome? If I recall, that is often linked to a neurodegenerative disease or vascular dementia.'

'Early onset Parkinson's she said. It seemed pretty tragic. Anyway, maybe it was murder? After all, Poppy did hot-wash some evidence yesterday.'

'I think the wine has gone to your head. We'd better eat?'

With a sheepish smile, Ramzi examined the menu on the table.

'Do you like oysters?' Rashida said.

To his horror, Ramzi heard himself say, 'Definitely—they're an aphrodisiac.'

'I didn't realise you had other plans for this evening?'

'Yes. I mean, no. I'm saying I like oysters, but in Marrakech, the desert, and so, the sea, well—'

Amused, Rashida said, 'Oysters are rich in zinc, which can boost your testosterone. Is that what you mean? To be on the safe side, we'd better order just the plate of half-dozen from Oulidia as an appetizer, and divide them?'

'Fine by me—'

Like a genie, a waiter appeared, noting the order.

'I'll have the linguini with clams.'

'For me: *Cassoulet de lapin de ma grand mère*. Thank you.'

'Which reminds me, Poppy said her grandmother had her dowry jewellery taken after they left the village.'

'The men lost their land and livelihood and the women lost their bridal jewellery. Do you know how valuable jewellery was, and still is, for women in parts of the world, as a symbol of marriage and family life? To say nothing of breakdown of community or village bonds.'

The oysters arrived on the plate arranged in a star. Six points. It reminded Ramzi of the town's stone carvings, Jewish symbols and pre-colonial national flags.

The oysters tasted briny, metallic and buttery, and the pasta a delight. As she polished off the dish of rabbit, Rashida's appetite never ceased to amaze him. Perhaps it was the crack-of-dawn call, the sea air, the windsurfing or—

'I have a fast metabolism,' she said, like a mind reader.

As agreed the night before, Ramzi paid. Rashida suggested a detour to show Ramzi the small square dedicated to Orson Welles, with the actor's face sculpted on a plaque, back-dropped by an angle of white battlements. They strolled through one stone gateway to another at Bab L'Magana, named after the high square clock tower. Beside it, they said goodnight. Meandering back to Riad Safsaf, Ramzi realized he had no idea where she was staying—why hadn't he asked?

Back in his room, Ramzi picked up the medjoul date from the paper case on the dish beside his bed. As he chewed, it sprung to mind that the night before, when he knocked against the nightstand in Spielman's room, there was no date in the petit four paper case nor on the dish.

As there were no locks on the doors, perhaps someone had sneaked in, removed the almond paste and put the powdered root of the Glue Thistle into the cavity. The colour and sweetness would have masked any taste, and by all accounts, the several glasses of *mahia* would exacerbate its effect.

Deciding to check his hypothesis he took a clean T-shirt and wrapped it round his right-hand in case of fingerprints, before checking the landing was clear. Despite being off limits, he crept into Spielberg's room, met by the faint chlorine-like smell of bleach. All was as it had been, including the bed covers thrown back and the dead man's clothes draped over the chair.

The nightstand was a different matter. No longer was there an empty paper case but one containing a medjoul date stuffed with almond paste. Beside it a black pillbox, the top overlaid with a gold bee. Neither item had been there the night before. Not only was the pillbox memorable, but when he had almost tipped the table and lamp over, Ramzi would have had to stop it sliding to the floor. Grabbing it with the T-shirt he pressed the catch. The lid sprang open. Inside were orange-green capsules—Spielman's angina medication.

THIRTEEN

A notification like the ping of a hotel desk bell roused him. Honestly, an online booking alert at six fifteen in the morning! Ramzi groaned. Why hadn't he flicked the phone to silent?

Rolling out of bed and making for the bathroom, he had a flash of inspiration. Pulling on swimming shorts, a T-shirt and trainers, he sat on the bed listening for any sign of the guests—or one in particular. Sure enough, a door opened. He quickly stepped out onto the landing, bumping into Oren.

'What a surprise!' Ramzi said. 'I was just off for a run before breakfast.'

'So was I. Care to join me?'

Outside, on the Place Moulay Hussain, they hesitated before deciding to head along the seafront on Boulevard Mohammed V and back through the new town to join the eastern ramparts of the old city.

Grey cumulus clouds sailed across a yellow sky. The sea shone as it lapped onto the sweeping bay. Panting a little, Ramzi already regretted this impetuous decision. Jogging past *Le Chalet de la Plage* restaurant, thoughts of Rashida and last night's dinner *à deux* jostled into his head. Despite the early hour, a young man lined up loungers on his beach concession. Elsewhere the profusion of thatched umbrellas in the shadowy light resembled displays of 1950s swing dresses on poles. Huts advertised windsurf and kitesurf schools along with equipment hire. An impression of Rashida popped up again. Beyond, two riders on horses seemed to gallop on air, the hooves shrouded by puffs of sand.

'Let's admire the view for a second,' Ramzi said. He flopped onto the broad-capped parapet, pretending to see something fascinating on the beach below, catching his breath. Meantime, Oren did push-ups on the promenade. Jumping up, he brushed dust and a few grains of sand from his hands.

'What a pity about Isaac Spielman,' Ramzi said at last, with a slight wheeze.

'Yes, it was.' Oren sat beside him, fit as a flea.

'I believe you were one of the last to speak to him at the *hillula*?'

'Who told you that?'

'Rachel—or was it Rebecca?' Ramzi said, with a small smile.

'Yes, we talked.'

'Did you know he was here? Is that why you came?'

'You ask a lot of questions.'

Ramzi tried to look surprised. 'Well, you both worked in construction. Though of course, he was much older than you.'

'Look, I came for the *hillula*, because I'm having difficulty finding projects to keep my company afloat. I thought I would ask the *tzaddik* for a sign or help. Well, imagine when I arrived: there was Isaac Spielman. I knew him by sight of course; he's been on television and in the business papers. More—he was staying at the same riad. I thought it was the sign I was looking for.'

'How exactly?

'Spielman, he was a war hero, older than me and work fell from the sky. Some say he received preferential treatment. Others say by other means.'

'Bribes?'

'You said it, not me,' Oren said as he burst into jumping jacks—where did he get the stamina? 'Of course, having contacts in government always helps, as it does in most countries.'

'Meaning his son, Levi?'

'And others. The point being, Spielman always had construction projects underway.'

'You wanted him to help?'

Oren halted. 'Look, I thought, this wasn't just a coincidence. I walked with him to the *hillula* and seemed to have hit it off. Then, just before the feast, one of the songs they sang, one of the lines, about deserving merit, recommended that we all:

Share passing wealth,
To deserve merit.'

'I couldn't believe it. I thought this was another sign. I saw him go to the washroom. When he came back to the banqueting hall, I cornered him, explaining that meeting here together and the song were signs from the *tzaddik* Rabbi Haim Pinto. I asked if he could help me by giving some construction work to my company, rather than grabbing every contract for himself.'

'*Sharing his passing wealth*—' Ramzi thought out loud.

'Exactly.'

'What was his reaction?'

'He was livid. In fact, he started being insulting—even threatening. I apologised, really shocked. Then, back at the table, he stonewalled me. I felt humiliated, and after what he said, a bit scared. I decided to leave, and back at the riad I met you and we had that glass of whisky on the roof terrace.'

'You were happy he was dead? Is that why you laughed?'

Oren shook his head. 'No. I laughed at the irony. Perhaps that was the sign I came for? Spielman dying will mean less work going his way. Even if the company goes on, his military heroism and status will stand for nothing. In fact, since neither of his sons are directly involved, it may close down.'

'So, Spielman dying here at the *hillula* is your sign.'

'Or maybe even a sign to him from the *tzaddik*, for coming back here.'

'Well his last words were something about returning.'

'You speak Hebrew?' Oren said, surprised.

'No, it was in English. Although he did keep repeating something in Hebrew before he died. *Teshu*—something.'

'*Teshuva*?' Oren suggested.

'That was the word, I'm sure.'

Oren laughed.

'Was he being witty on his deathbed?' Ramzi asked.

'*Teshuva* means "to repent". The literal meaning of *shuva* is "to return" or "returning". We believe righteousness is a man's natural state and sinfulness is unnatural. When a person repents he is returning to that natural state. When doing *teshuva*, one "returns" to his previous deeds to make amends. He wanted to repent, but it seems it was too late.'

'Of course,' Ramzi said. 'The word "returning" was perhaps the best he could conjure up in his state.'

FOURTEEN

Jelly-legged, Ramzi staggered like a drunk into his room to collapse on the bed. Catching his breath, he recalled what Rebecca and Rachel said about Spielman threatening to report Oren's company for a fatal construction accident and alert the media. No doubt, that would harm a fledgling company. Was this merely the *mahia* spirit talking or had Spielman threatened him face-to-face earlier at the banquet? A jingle interrupted his thoughts.

Oh jeez—a call!

'Hisham?'

'How are you Mr. Ramzi? Your breathing is very loud.'

'I was running to the phone.' To a degree.

'It must be nice getting up late and not doing a thing at Riad Safsaf.'

'That was the idea—'

'Have you been on a camel ride on the beach?'

'Not yet. Is everything okay? You sound upset.'

'Mr. Ramzi, the debt collector wrote. It's a lie that you told me to lie! This might ruin our reputation as a business!'

'Thank you Hisham. I will check the mail and deal with it.'

'Thank you Mr. Ramzi.

'Say hello to Latifa for me.'

'Latifa wants you to check the labels on the bed linen and towels in your room in Essaouira.'

'Sure. But why?'

'She can only work with top quality bedding and towels.'

'But they are! The towels are 650 grams per square metre and the sheets are Egyptian Cotton 550 threads—they cost a small fortune.'

'Not according to Latifa. "Cheap and crummy," were her words. It appears the towels in Riad Aztra along the lane are always fluffy. She called you a skinflint, by the way. She's beside me. Shall I hand you across?'

Terror-struck, Ramzi gasped out, 'I think the debt collector is the priority!'

'All right, but don't forget a photo.'

'A photo? Of the labels?'

'No. Of you on the camel ride. Latifa! Let go of my phone, you'll make me drop it! He's busy, I tell you. Ow, that really hurt—'

Cutting the call, Ramzi slumped against the pillows, searching his mobile for the offending e-mail. Having found it, he read:

> *I generally encourage negotiations. If you feel able to talk to Ryan, please do. Everything should be 'without prejudice.'*
> *However, when I rang him he made all sorts of allegations of fraud, a cover up, an insurance scam (I think) and a request by you for the manager to lie. You may want to record the conversation lest it amounts to blackmail. I suppose he may intend to threaten all sorts of publicity.*

I think… That inspired confidence. He certainly wasn't going to phone, risk a shouting match, and a mega bill as well. He'd pen a reply later to keep matters documented. For the moment, he was more alarmed by Latifa's whims and fancies and Hisham's photo request.

Washed and dressed, he made for the roof terrace. The debris of breakfast in front of her, Abigail flicked a polished fingernail up and down over her phone. Seeing Ramzi, she smiled.

'Good morning. Are you alright? You look one way but your legs walk another.'

'Oh, just a little early morning exercise.'

'Why not join me?'

Ramzi pulled up a chair. He glanced warily at the seagulls overhead.

'They're intelligent birds. Did you know they use bread crumbs to attract fish? Another thing is that they use their feet to produce a sound like rain to attract earthworms hidden under the ground.'

'I can imagine. One stole butter from my dish the other day, but didn't warn me first by tap-dancing.'

Abigail laughed. 'They're also good at facial recognition, so it may come back.'

'Tomorrow I'll wear a false beard and baseball cap.'

'Stop making me laugh. Someone might arrive and think it disrespectful.'

'How is your husband?'

'Yitzak? Okay, considering. He didn't really want to come, but hadn't seen his father for a while. To be honest, we were and we are the black sheep of the family.

'I don't mean to be rude, but is it because he married you? Are you Jewish?'

'Yes, from Philadelphia.'

'Right. He said his brother lived in Israel. Was Yitzak the black sheep by living in the States?'

She smiled. 'You do ask a lot of questions.'

The same comment, twice before breakfast!

'No. It's more complicated than that,' Abigail said. 'Yitzak was a *refusenik*.'

Just as the twins had said.

'A *refusenik*. In the sense of refusing to be conscripted into the military?'

'Exactly. I am sure you can imagine his father's reaction.'

'The decorated war hero. I can.'

'Excuse me.' Youssef tidied the table, laying a breakfast for Ramzi.

'No butter today, thanks.'

'Yes sir.'

He put an ornate silver teapot beside him.

'Sorry, Youssef, could I have coffee instead of tea?'

'The coffee jar was empty when I came this morning. I take my day off and everything goes to pieces.' He shrugged. 'What can I do?'

Butter back on the tray, he returned downstairs. Ramzi gave Abigail a bewildered look.

'I know,' Abigail said, shaking her head. 'He's got a bit of an attitude.'

'You were saying?'

'I was about to comment, that as for me, I am beyond the pale.'

'I can't believe that,' Ramzi said.

She laughed. 'I work with the Jewish Voice for Peace. As American Jews, we support the aspirations of Israelis and Palestinians for self-determination.'

'Sounds like a tall order.'

'Ending the occupation of the West bank, Gaza and East Jerusalem and all violence against civilians? Justice for Palestinians? It is, but we're in it for the long haul.'

'Your father-in-law disagreed with this?'

'You have no idea. Of course, it's concerned with the Jewish settlements on the Occupied Territories. He'd been involved in their construction, you see.'

'I do see. I imagine those conversations livened up family dinners.'

A sadness clouded Abigail's face. 'Have you been to Israel?'

'No.'

'Personally, I find the country disturbing. The first time I visited it was a shattering experience. Everything seemed an illusion—'

'In what ways?'

'Take for instance the national parks. They were created by government's Jewish National Fund across the sites of many Palestinian villages that Israel eradicated—'.

'During the Nakba—'

'And afterwards. Hundreds of thousands orange and olive trees were ripped out. Some of the olive trees were two to three hundred years old. Traces of Ottoman, Arab and Palestinian life were razed to the ground. All this helped promote the myth of Palestine as an empty and arid country until Israel became a state. Then Israel planted over the bulldozed villages, the fields, the orchards and the olive groves.'

'It sounds like a way of saying, "We are here".'

'Exactly. And, "You never were." But instead of indigenous flora, the government, for the most part, opted for pines and cypress trees to create a European landscape—one argument was that it supported the wood industry. Well, you may or may not know, pine needles create acidic ground cover, making it inhospitable to other plant species or animals and impossible to farm. What they created are known as pine deserts—nice irony, don't you think?'

'Apart from being difficult to return the land to agriculture, it sounds a disaster in terms of biodiversity. Were they used to produce wood?'

'Recreation, for the most part. Forest parks became walking trails, picnic spots and children's playgrounds, with commemorative stones or memorials to the holocaust, ghetto resistance fighters, to Anne Frank, or to the revival of the nation of Israel. Here and there, a ruined house, a piece of pottery, and a heroic fig or almond tree is all that survives of the Palestinian past. But it goes beyond that, beyond borders. Where we live in Philadelphia we often see a food truck. On the side, it advertises *Israeli inspired cuisine*. Hummus, falafel, shawarma. The foods originated in the Middle East and Turkey well before Israel existed. Not only are Israel annexing land and homes, but taking Palestinian heritage and culture and promoting it as their own.'

'You should talk to Poppy. Or better not: it'll only upset her. I'm terrified to criticise Israel in case someone thinks I'm antisemitic.'

'Are you serious?' For a spell, Abigail played with the chunky beads of her necklace, then leant forward. 'Of course, antisemitism exists. But, everyone is free to criticise or reject anything to do with the State of Israel or its government, and that includes their policies toward Palestinian territory. After all, Israeli citizens do. The world is free to find fault with America, Britain, China, Egypt or any other country, so why not Israel as well? Condemning Israel and being in favour of the Palestinian cause is not automatically hateful towards Jews and not necessarily a form of antisemitism.'

'Not all Jews are Zionists then, judging from what you say?'

'No. To believe otherwise is a mistake. The idea that all Jews have the same beliefs and political commitments? To me, *that* is antisemitic. Worse, it also suggests that in America and elsewhere, the loyalty of Jews like myself is to a foreign government and their real home is Israel. All this plays into the belief that we can't truly belong in our own homelands, or become a part of their societies and communities. My family are Sephardic and emigrated from Brazil to New York back in the eighteenth century, well before American independence. We are American to the core. My grandmother is older than Israel and she has no wish to go or visit there—Forgive me, I hope I'm not lecturing you?'

'Not at all. I like your passion,' Ramzi said, his mind drifting. His physics lectures had a reputation as being passionate before he took the open-ended sabbatical from the university. Being September, the new semester would be soon starting, yet—

'Are you okay?'

Ramzi snapped back to the present. 'Sorry Abigail! Yes, all that seems logical to me. Thank you. Now, am I throwing a hand grenade if I mention The Wall?'

She sat back. 'The Separation Wall? No, not at all. Silence is complicity, don't you think? Yitzak's father was involved in building it, and that makes me ashamed. Can you imagine military checkpoints being part of a daily routine? This is what happens for almost three million Palestinians. It prevents freedom of movement, affects the right to work, to medical care—ambulances and patients often cannot reach hospitals—the right to education, to social services and a minimal standard of living. For all those reasons and more, in case you didn't know, back in 2004 or so, the International Court of Justice advised that it was unlawful. Quite honestly, it breaks my heart and I wish it could be brought down.'

'The pictures I've seen—it's as high as the riads here in Essaouira—three stories, that's maybe eight metres, and like a concrete snake.'

'A snake and a deadly one at that. It'll be seven hundred kilometres long, double the length of the 'Green Line', which was the 1967 pre-occupation border. It twists and turns, cutting deep into Palestinian territory, confiscating swathes of fertile Palestinian land, most of its water resources, and breaking down urban and rural ties that go back centuries.

'Naturally, all this reinforces the majority of the Israel's illegal settlements, ensuring they can expand, much to my late father-in-law's delight. Imagine his reaction when we tried to tell him how it poisons both

Israel and Palestine, and their people's lives. Even our family's lives. Oh, here's Zak—'

'I was speaking to Levi. He's arranging our father's residence certificate in Tel Aviv so that the National Insurance Institute will pay his customs clearance and burial fees.'

'Customs clearance?' Ramzi asked, incredulous.

'Yes,' Yitzak said, sitting down. 'I'm not sure if they will deny his entry on the grounds of being a collectable coin, a medical sample or something radioactive. Probably the latter.'

'Would you like some tea?' Abigail asked her husband.

'Thank you,' Ramzi said, quickly passing his cup. It was no time to make a discreet departure.

Taken aback, Abigail poured for both her husband and Ramzi.

'You were saying your father was a nuclear hazard?' Ramzi prompted.

Yitzak tore a piece off a croissant. 'That's one way of putting it. He was toxic. I'd had my fill of being stonewalled and ignored by him. Well, now he'll be silent for good.'

'He was a bully?' Ramzi prodded, recalling the conversation he had overheard.

'And how! I don't hear from him for two years. My calls and messages—ignored. Why? Because, like Abigail and millions of others, I want a different Israel. Then, out of the blue, he invites us to join him on the *hillula*. Take a running jump! That was my first thought, but Abigail talked me into coming. It's easy now our sons are both in college. We flew to Lisbon and then on to Marrakech for a couple of nights, to adjust to the time zone before taking the bus here. However, what happens on Day One? Well, he said, "Let's meet at 9.30 for breakfast" and then insisted he said 8.30. We arrived late for breakfast, so he ignored us. Typical—my mother was also used to that. "Thursday? No silly, I said Saturday." "Meet our friends at the *Popina* restaurant? No, I said at the *Dallal*." He was always accusing her of saying things that she hadn't.'

'Gaslighting, in a word.'

'Yes. If my mother had seen my aunt blown up in a terrorist attack he would have said "No—she spontaneously combusted."'

'Yitzak!'

'Okay, that was in bad taste. Anyhow, one of her friends suggested my mother kept a diary, so she did. It didn't take her long to find that he was distorting reality and she wasn't going slowly insane. As soon as we were old enough she left him.'

'He seemed pleasant enough to me. He showed me round the Mellah—what's left of it.'

'Of course, turning on the charm is part of his success, but he hated criticism—'

'*Monsieur*?'

Youssef stood beside him.

'Inspector Hassani would like to see you downstairs when you have finished breakfast.'

Abigail exchanged a look with Yitzak.

'Okay we'll come in a second. Apologies if I got on my hobby horse earlier.'

'Not at all, Abigail. It was all very illuminating.'

They stood up, and Youssef started to clear the table.

'Good morning! Are you leaving?' Rebecca said.

'The Inspector is here. About the autopsy I imagine,' Yitzak replied.

'Don't forget to see the photos I took of the *hillula*.'

'I forgot to ask. Did you show them to Inspector Hassani?' Ramzi said. He turned to Yitzak. 'If your father didn't die of natural causes they could contain a clue.'

'You mean he might have been murdered—?' Yitzak said.

'Murdered, yes,' Ramzi said.

'How silly of me. I didn't think,' Rebecca said. 'My shots are all at bit dull really, but I found one or two of your father Yitzak, if it's not too painful?'

'No, that's fine. Thanks. I'll look later.'

Youssef piled some plates. After he left the terrace, Rebecca said, 'I see the Inspector has called in reinforcements.'

Abigail and Yitzak looked alarmed.

'How do you know?' Ramzi said.

'Youssef's latest baseball cap. Didn't you see the brand? NYPD—New York Police Department.'

FIFTEEN

Ramzi hovered around Riad Safsaf to find out what Inspector Hassani wanted. A murmur of voices came from the salon. As the door was shut, standing sentry would not be subtle, so he ran back upstairs to the first-floor landing.

Poised to pounce from his room, the wait for news got the better of him. Giving up, he rolled a towel round a book and sun tan lotion. On aching leg muscles, he retraced his path that morning to the beach, now busy with visitors. After hiring a lounger, Ramzi rubbed on Factor 30 and stretched out in the sun. His book focused on the friendship between Carl Jung and the quantum physicist, Nobel laureate Wolfgang Pauli, and their search for the meaning of the prime number 137 in science, their interest in medieval alchemy, as well as dream interpretation.

The Atlantic breeze made the morning pleasant, but soon the swirls of fine sand stuck to his skin and his hair. He decided to rinse it off with a plunge in the sea, his skin gently sandblasted on the way. Around him people waded into the shallows in bikinis, burkinis, flowing kaftans, speedos, trunks, and pyjamas. As dying waves lapped over his feet, he watched the windsurfers at the far end of the bay. Narrowing his eyes, he was unable to make out if one happened to be Rashida. Finally, splashing water on the back of his neck, he dived in to wash off the sand.

Gasping at the cold, he rapidly waded out again. The salt water felt stickier and the flights of sand more abrasive.

Giving up, Ramzi collected his things, trudging back towards Riad Safsaf. Along the way he decided to take a slight detour to see the esplanade of canopied tables glittering with displays of fish and seafood. Approaching the waterfront, he stood mesmerised by two fishing smacks, pulled up a slipway to dry dock, their keel plates set on timber blocks. Further on, a square stone tower, bartizans overhanging the four corners, dominated the port. Blue feluccas packed the harbour, some with oars, others with outboard motors, overshadowed by three or four trawlers and a sky vibrant with whirling seagulls. Against their calls, the sea and the wind, he heard a woman shout his name.

Ramzi turned to see Rachel—and nearby her sister in an acrobatic position, pointing a camera at the vessels.

'Hello again.'

'I hope the *Tubi 60* didn't give you a sore head. It shouldn't.'

'The *Tubi 60* didn't,' Ramzi smiled. 'But the *Krav Maga* on the other hand…'

Rachel laughed. 'Join us,' she said.

'Great,' Ramzi said, not believing his luck.

'Are you sure? You seem to be hobbling?'

'I went running. A bit out of condition. I must have a few kilos of sand stuck to me from the beach.'

'Can we go this way?'

They ambled through the tower onto the *Sqala du Port*, the sea walls once again, lined with cannons.

'Essaouira was certainly well defended,' Rachel commented.

To avoid other mundane comments, Ramzi suggested they sit for a bit, gesturing to a stone bench set into the harbour wall, the winches and wheelhouses of the trawlers looming behind it. Rebecca's photographic gymnastics continued as she headed into the distance, turning to focus her camera on two fishing boats ploughing through the sea, towards the harbour.

'You mentioned the Jewish Community in Casablanca? An article you were writing?'

'It's for the *Jerusalem Post*, about the people left behind.'

'Left behind?'

'Casablanca was a departure point for Moroccan Jews to Israel. But the passage was refused to the sick, and physically or mentally disabled.'

'That's quite a surprise. I mean, considering the persecution of people with disabilities in the Third Reich. Weren't they called, *lives unworthy of life*?'

'Exactly, the drive for an Aryan master race. But this screening of the fittest migrants started during the British Mandate for Palestine before the establishment of the State of Israel, with a similar *raison d'être*: the sick would be a burden on the country's resources.'

'And the policy continued?' Ramzi asked, taken aback.

'It fitted in with Zionist ideology to create a new Jewish nation, healthy in body and mind. As you may imagine, this was a reaction to the awful stereotypes directed at Jews in European culture. Often, they portrayed the Jews as having physical, genetic or mental disabilities.'

'So, in a nutshell, presuming them an inferior race.'

'More or less. The Zionist movement worked to transform the Jewish image—grotesque caricatures aside—from someone pale, sick, weak and feminine into a person who was healthy, beautiful, strong and masculine. As you can see, it really was a reaction to those stereotypes, because this new image advocated all sorts of things, such as productivity, physical labour, self-defence and security—all in all a vision of the Jews as an earthly, self-sufficient and productive nation. This required a certain type of person who was, how can I put it? A fighter-worker. So back then, it was vital that an immigrant had no disability that limited their work capacity in any way. Therefore, the blind, those with handicaps, and illnesses such as tuberculosis were turned away.'

'And that explains the people left behind?'

'Well, here's the contradiction. In Israel in 1950, The Law of Return was enacted. It begins by declaring that *Every Jew has the right to come to this country as an Oleh. Oleh* is the term for a Jewish immigrant to Israel. The migration itself is called the *Aliyah.*

'*Aliyah* Emissaries searched for Jewish families, including those from Morocco, willing and able to relocate. The families had to help with the construction and settlement of Israel.'

'I see. And some were deemed, shall I say, "unsuitable"?'

'That's a diplomatic way of putting it, Ramzi, but ultimately, yes. Some were physically or mentally impaired. Some might have had a genetic condition such as Down's syndrome. Even their physical appearance could rule them out, for instance, if they had too small a skull.'

'Sounds like a controversial piece—'

'That's just part of it, though. Take the tale of Avraam, one of the Moroccan Jews that came up in our research. The family planned to emigrate to Israel and he was eight at the time. His sister Hanina described him as being restless, fidgety and forever talking or interrupting conversations. Nowadays, that might have been diagnosed as attention deficit hyperactivity disorder.'

'ADHD? I've heard of it.'

'That's it. Nevertheless, he was mandated to stay behind. His family stayed in Casablanca too, as they couldn't bear to leave him, though Hanina, emigrated to Israel a few years later. In fact, she was the one who contacted me in Israel about Avraam and this story.

'Now, the intriguing question is, what could the *Aliyah* Emissary who came at dawn to the family's house have known about him? Where did that knowledge come from? Was the data on the family collected without their consent or full understanding, and if so, from where? A doctor? Neighbours? Or was it an ad hoc decision based on a first impression?'

'I can see the implications. What happened to Avraam?'

'For many people ADHD is for life. However, he was one of the children that more or less outgrew it. Most of his symptoms disappeared after puberty. Eventually, he became a teacher at a French elementary school in Casablanca. Perfect really. He had a dynamic personality, could think on his feet and move from task-to-task quickly. He's retired no—'

'Goodness! The two of you seem deep in conversation?' Rebecca smiled, approaching them.

'We were just talking about our article.'

'Avraam's story,' Ramzi said. 'It sounds like compulsive reading. I had no idea about the selection. I am sure some people will find it pretty upsetting.'

'That's the point,' Rebecca frowned.

'Talking of upsetting matters, I was about to ask, why did you think Spielman was poisoned?'

'You do ask a lot of questions!' the twins chimed in unison

What—three strikes in a morning!

Rebecca thrust her camera's LCD screen towards them. 'Look at these photos I took.'

Kudos given, they walked back, stopping to see crates of fish offloaded by a human conveyor belt across the feluccas, creating rainbow stacks on the quay—another perfect photo opportunity for Rebecca. Here, Ramzi made his excuses, and continued on alone.

SIXTEEN

Taking his book on Jung and Pauli, Ramzi hoped it might be more pleasant to continue it on a lounger on the roof terrace. Ester had the same idea with a novel, and lay in a swimming costume, stretched out reading.

'Hello Ester. Good book?'

'A murder mystery. Not as intellectual as yours—I see the number 137 on the cover. The fine structure constant.'

Ramzi sat on the empty lounger beside her. 'Pauli was obsessed with it his whole life. In fact, he joked that when he died his first question to the Devil would be: what is the meaning of the fine structure constant?'

Ester laughed. 'I rather imagine 137 would be the number you'd signal to aliens to show we had some mastery over our planet and understood quantum mechanics. The aliens would know that integer as well, as they must have developed advanced sciences. And did you know 137 is the numeric value of the Hebrew word Kabbalah?'

'Linking physics and mysticism. And did you know Pauli died in room 137 of the hospital in Zurich?'

'In some ways, that's not surprising.'

'What I do find surprising is seeing you here. I thought you were *persona non-grata*?'

Ester put her paperback on the side table. 'As the Inspector took our passports, Poppy had to retract her ultimatum.'

'The threat to kill you?' Ramzi said.

'You overheard? Well, I did drop a bombshell, so understand her being so upset.'

'May I ask—?'

'It's no secret. This riad—that she called Safsaf—belonged, or should I say, belongs to my family.'

'You're not here for the *hillula*?'

'It was a good opportunity. Killing two birds with one stone.'

'Forgive my ignorance, but if your family were Jews, didn't they have to live in the Mellah?'

'According to family history, at the beginning of the nineteenth century all sorts of minor incidents happened here in Essaouira—Mogador as it was known then—between the Jewish and Muslim community. To regain the peace, the sultan, Moulay Slimane, decreed in 1807 that a new Mellah be built for the Jews.'

'To the north-east, by the Bab Doukkala gateway. I saw the remains of the neighbourhood with Spielman. A collapsing ghetto.'

'Tragic, isn't it? That's what it became after the mass exodus to Israel. Anyhow, the Mellah was finished in 1809 and the Jewish Community were relocated. In effect, they switched zones with the Muslims. Everyone knew it would happen, but not when. Without notice, the order came and it took place all in a rush one Saturday—the Sabbath—which in our faith, is our day of rest.'

'Sounds like total chaos!' Ramzi cried out.

'By all accounts it was.'

'How did it work? Did they swap their homes like for like or were they compensated?'

'Officially, the Sultan promised to compensate them. However, they based this on the price offered by the eventual buyer. Of course, the buyers were the town's Muslim Community and, overall, the price they offered amounted to only about a sixth of a property's value. On top of this, the land they were built on belonged to the Sultan and he pocketed a third of each estimated price, leaving the rest for the Jewish owner.'

'One ninth of the value,' Ramzi calculated.

'That's about it. Anyway, the Sultan made an exception for a handful of families, known as the *Toujjar as-Sultan*, who were rich, independent merchants. This created a type of Jewish aristocracy in the late eighteenth century. Our family's name was Guédalla, and one of the ten *Toujjar.* As the Sultan's Merchants, there came various privileges, such as being able to borrow capital, receive tax exemptions, as well as being under the protection of the Sultan, with a guard of two soldiers at their disposal. Oh, and they also got two African slaves as gifts.'

'How times have changed, thank heavens—'

'I agree. It doesn't bear thinking about—not in the twenty-first century in any case. Now, where was I? Ah yes, over and above those privileges, it was possible to keep living in the Kasbah, the quarter where we are now. On their death, the title would pass on to their son. If the family died out or left, the current Sultan would appoint another *Tajer* to join the Sultan's *Toujjar* of merchants. So, because my ancestor held the title of *Tajer As-Sultan,* he bought this riad—it was said to be one of the loveliest houses in Essaouira. Of course, because of its height, at that time it had a view that let my ancestors be amongst the first to spot merchant ships and also, being so near the port it had advantages for trading.

Mind you, that was a hundred years before the Protectorate and the growth of Casablanca and its port.

'You may not have noticed, but above the front door to the riad is a six-petal flower carved onto the stone—it represents the Seal of Solomon. In fact, the merchandise was stored in the courtyard and the rooms off it. The family lived on the two stories above.

'Well, fast forward to 1963 and changed times. My family left on the second May. A Thursday. It was the biggest Jewish emigration from the town in a single day: 350 people taken on seven busses to Casablanca. There they boarded a Greek merchant ship that sailed to Marseille, and from there, on to Israel.

'However, even though they left Morocco, my family rented out the riad through an accountant, but as time went on, the payments petered out. We were pretty philosophical about it, out of sight out of mind, and all that, but a few months ago, we heard the riad had been sold, and to Poppy. One of the neighbours, found out after the sale, but nevertheless, contacted us.'

'Did the property have a land title?'

'Legally, it remained as a *melkia*.'

'That's the problem,' Ramzi said. 'Most old properties in Marrakech are the same since a *melkia* has a legal value, but it does not give the precise footprint of the property nor the number of legal successors. I would say that to safeguard the purchase the buyer really needs to apply for a *titre foncier*. Legally, it becomes inalienable.'

'Quite right. But part of the process to lay claim to this is the requisition, which is still undergoing. When he left, my grandfather took the original *melkia* title deed with him and the leasing agreement. After getting advice from our notary, we are arguing that technically the riad is still ours, as it was already inalienable.'

The two of them sat in silence for a moment, before Ester went on.

'After I arrived I explained this to Poppy. She called me a liar. When she did, I pointed to the courtyard.'

'The courtyard?'

'Yes: you can take up those two central stones. And beneath them is a secret cellar where valuables were hidden and that spirit, *mahia* was brewed. Even Poppy didn't know about that.'

'What about the *jidwel*. Do you think Poppy made it to scare you away?'

'It's plausible, but would she know what a *jidwel* was—or indeed, know Hebrew?'

'Presuming not, I imagine it was aimed at Spielman? Or was his death a coincidence?'

'I know, for a fact, it wasn't meant for Spielman.'

'What!'

'I hope I'm not interrupting anything?' Abigail said, strolling onto the terrace.

'Well, actually—' Ramzi began.

'Did you get to speak to Inspector Hassani this morning?' Ester asked.

'We did and he was very apologetic for the delay on the decision for an autopsy. It seems the Moroccan authorities are in a quandary over the matter. Deciding to bury him in Israel has hardly helped matters.'

'In Israel?'

'Yes. A combination of religious reasons and having a military honour guard fire a salute.'

'Our national war hero.' Standing, Ester wrapped her waist with a sarong, and scooped up the novel. 'I think I'll freshen up before this evening. I imagine you and Yitzak won't be coming to the final celebrations tonight?'

'Why think that? Without my father-in-law, I think I'll really enjoy them.'

SEVENTEEN

'Why are you waddling like a duck?'

Keen as Ramzi was to pursue Ester's news on the *jidwel*, he'd needed to shower off the morning at the beach before meeting Rashida. They had just arrived at *Le Chalet de la Plage*, shown to a table with a sea view. Ramzi tried to explain about the morning run with Oren.

'Maybe I could be a stand-up comedian, judging by your reaction,' he said.

'Well, was it worth it?'

'Yes, in fact. But I don't think I'll tell you.'

'Oh please,' Rashida said. 'I'll be good.'

Ramzi lost no time explaining about the reason.

'Well, money is a good motive for murder,' Rashida said. 'If Spielman died, perhaps more construction projects would come his way, especially without the aura of a war hero tipping the balance when it came to awarding contracts.'

'That's what he implied. Still poisoning seems farfetched. One never knows, Spielman could have reflected on what Oren said, and changed his mind overnight.'

'Coming back to what Oren told me about *teshuva*, or repentance, I doubt he would have time to repent.'

'I am sure it was meant in the wider context.'

'Then there was my drink with Oren on the night Spielman died. He needed to calm down after being insulted. Besides, he told me he came for a sign from the *tzaddik* Haim Pinto. I don't think choosing to poison him could be seen as a sign.'

'Ester left the *hillula* dinner too.'

'I think we could rule her out. She told me she came to claim ownership of Riad Safsaf.'

'Tell me more—'

Ramzi related the conversation about Ester and her family history.

'I'm not really understanding who sent the *jidwel* to Ester and why? If it was Poppy?'

'A case of history repeating itself?' Rashida said. 'Poppy's property seized on the basis of "we lived there once and were promised it?" It's a bit like looking in a distorting mirror at a carnival.'

'I wanted to run after her. Abigail, that is—but I needed to shower before meeting you.'

'I'm flattered, but didn't realize you want to run after other women.'

Blushing, Ramzi suggested they order, in the end, sharing a sea food gratin, followed by a sole, and a bottle of Moroccan *Medaillon* sauvignon blanc.

'Maybe it was Poppy,' he said, after the wine arrived. 'I'm surprised that it was in Hebrew. Of course, don't forget I overheard her threatening to kill Ester. Why make a *jidwel* to cast a spell, and then threaten her in person?'

'Fair point.'

'Who is more interesting is Abigail, his darling daughter-in-law. She works for the Jewish Voice for Peace.'

'The American organization? I've heard of it.'

'Supporting Palestine and condemning Israeli settlements. She was pretty incensed.'

After listening to Ramzi's account, Rashida said. 'I'm reminded of Ikkyu the Japanese monk. Fourteenth Century.'

'Now we're in Japan. That's a bit random.'

'Sorry about the jetlag.' She flashed him a smile. 'As I was saying, he wrote,

Fill the path
with fallen needles

of the pine tree
so that no-one knows if anyone lives there.'

'I didn't know you were so Zen. Maybe it's the Essaouira vibe?'

'I used to read Manga as a teenager—still do.'

The waiter brought the gratin.

'This smells delicious. As if this wasn't enough, Yitzak the *refusenik* confessed to him and his mother being bullied one way or another. And after their humiliation at the *hillula* dinner—' Ramzi said

'The idea of arriving in Morocco and immediately sourcing a poison, I don't think that likely. Flying over for a religious event with the purpose to murder?'

'Wait though. Abigail told me they spent two nights in Marrakech before heading down.'

'First stop, Rabba Lakdima, The Spice Trader's Square. I'm not really convinced,' Rashida said. 'How's the gratin?

'Excellent, thanks. I think the twin sisters can also be ruled out. They are journalists, though quite critical of the circumstances of "the left behind," as they call them'.

'Who are?'

Ramzi took a swallow of wine, and related the story they researched in Casablanca.

Finally, Rashida nodded. 'The boy you mentioned was fortunate to outgrow it. Nowadays there are treatments. Stimulants like amphetamines and non-stimulants. But it's a process of trial and error, complicated by genetics, side-effects, metabolism. Diet can help too. Still, I do find the cursory diagnosis is rather shocking.'

'In a way, I wasn't surprised after Spielman told me how the Sephardic Jews were insulted when they reached Israel. Come to think of it, maybe Rebecca and Rachel are not as innocent as they seem? After all, they escorted Spielman back to the riad.'

'Now you're guessing. What is their motive? Also, from what you said, a knockout blow from their combat training could have been easier?'

'Okay, I agree. If we're chasing down a murderer we're not much further forward. But I almost forgot. There's another thing.'

'Go on—'

'When Spielman was dying, I almost knocked over the nightstand. The riad leaves a complimentary medjoul date stuffed with almond paste by the bed. The paper case was empty, so Spielberg must have eaten it. The Glue Thistle could have been disguised as the paste.'

'That fits,' Rashida said. 'We know all the guests either came back early or escorted him to his room. It would have been easy to substitute one date for another.'

'Dare I confess, but there's more. I know I shouldn't have but I checked his room last night. A date was in the dish on the table, just as if he hadn't eaten it. Also, a pillbox with his angina capsules inside. That also wasn't on the table that night.'

'Well this is all excellent. Let's hope the autopsy gets the green light. Have some more wine, you deserve it. You certainly asked a lot of questions.'

Ramzi's brows furrowed. 'Strange. You are not the first to say that today.'

For a moment, Rashida looked at the orange sky over the darkening sea, before turning back to Ramzi.

'Be careful,' she said.

EIGHTEEN

Brushing his teeth, Ramzi's thoughts turned to Marrakech and the riad. He felt he had to stay in Essaouira whilst Spielman's death stayed a mystery, though maybe it would remain so? Also, it seemed a pity to leave with Rashida here on holiday. Although Ramzi dealt with any booking enquiries, he felt a degree of guilt at abandoning Hisham and Latifa to run the riad alone in Marrakech.

About to climb into bed, he remembered to check which company provided the linen, hoping to clear his conscience—and pacify Latifa. Ramzi turned up the corner of the mattress-cover under the pillows, but saw no tag. Untucking the bottom corner of the bed he found a label but, before he could begin reading it, saw something move. Throwing back the sheets, he discovered a small yellow creature with a pair of grasping pincers and a tail curved over its back.

Leaping back, he stood paralysed for a few seconds. A scorpion! Aha! Slowly, he opened his cabin-sized suitcase, took out a biro, scooped the clothes from the interior and slid the case under the edge of the bed. Pushing the arachnid off the mattress with a flip of the pen, it fell into the case. With a click, Ramzi snapped the lid shut.

Heart racing, down on his hands and knees he double-checked the beast had gone and emptied out his trainers. One by one, he pulled all the covers right back over the bed, shaking out the pillows.

He dialled Rashida.

'Ramzi? These late calls are becoming a habit.'

'I found a scorpion in my bed.'

'Did it sting you?' Rashida asked, quite matter-of-fact.

'No. What would have happened if it had?'

'Depends on the species. They are more lethal to children than to old men like you.'

'What! Old! I'm only—

'I'm joking. About your age, that is. Around eighty per cent of scorpion deaths are people under fifteen.'

'I almost wish I had been stung. You might have been more sympathetic.'

'I'd have come right over.'

'And—?'

'As a fan of traditional medicine, I'd have made a small incision, pulverised the venom with cold cooking gas, and put some raw garlic or honey on it. Maybe a splash of ammonia if there was some in the cleaning cupboard.'

'You are not taking this seriously.'

'Tell that to farming communities out in the country. For future reference, I have an anti-venom jab in my bag of tricks. Scorpions like burrowing into the dunes around Essaouira.'

'I hope it's a one off.'

'I'd do what many people do and write a charm to paste over the door to your room to scare them off. Where is it now?'

'In my suitcase.'

'Sweet! You've become friends. Are you taking it to Marrakech?'

'Good night.'

'Sweet dreams!'

Had she been laughing? Bewildered, Ramzi returned to the matter at hand. He recalled the crumbling building adjacent to Riad Safsaf. From the roof terrace, he could toss the beast into it. Still in his boxer shorts he grabbed the case and headed up the stairs.

Seeing the terrace door ajar he hesitated, hearing voices.

'Now we can put that money back in the boys' college funds,' Abigail said. 'Things will have to change Zak. This can't happen again.'

'Now my father's dead I feel like it's a new beginning.'

'It had better be. You can thank me for that.'

At the scrape of chairs on the tiles, Ramzi turned and hurried back down. Worried he might be seen if Abigail and Yitzak followed, he settled on Plan B—go downstairs to hurl the scorpion into the alleyway.

At the front door, Poppy popped out of the office.

'Monsieur Ramzi. What are you doing at the front door with a suitcase in your underwear? Are you slinking off? I don't believe you've paid your bill.'

Shaking himself, Ramzi widened his eyes.

'Good heavens! I must have been sleepwalking. Thank goodness you were still here! I'm surprised, it's so late.'

'I was talking to my brother in Quebec. Would you like me to barricade you in your room for your own safety?'

NINETEEN

Ramzi woke to the call of dawn prayer. The scorpion! Springing out of bed, he grabbed the suitcase, raced up the stairs to the terrace door, quietly turned the key, and by the parapet, unclipped the case to jettison the beast into the ruin next door.

Mission completed, he headed back to his room, empty suitcase in hand. Now for a lie in. Climbing between the scorpion-free sheets, it was bliss!

'Mr. Ramzi. Wake up!'

A woman's voice. Was he dreaming? He looked at his watch. 6.30 am.

'Just a minute,' he said throwing back the covers and grabbing some clothes.

Rebecca stood at the door, wrapped in a cotton dressing gown.

'Is everything alright? Come in—'

'Someone's taken—maybe stolen—my camera.'

A sense of déjà vu swept over him.

'Are you sure? You haven't mislaid it in the riad or at last night's celebrations?'

'No. Rachel persuaded me not to take it and just have a relaxing night. I should have known better as there's no key for any door here.'

'What can I do?'

'We—I mean, I—thought that as you run a riad in Marrakech, you could advise us—I mean me—how to handle things?'

Now he was a consultant!

'For instance, will the riad insurance cover it? And for my insurance, do I have to report it?'

Not again—!

'I would mention the camera went missing to Youssef and Poppy. Maybe they stumbled across it and locked it away in the safe, if they have one. Take it from there. Were all your photos on it?'

'Only a few from yesterday. Fortunately, I downloaded everything from Casablanca and the *hillula*. They're on my laptop and up in the clouds somewhere.'

'Well that is fortunate. Maybe someone was after the pictures rather than the camera.'

'Do you think so? How thrilling! Let's go and see.'

Ramzi followed her to the room.

'What bad luck' Rachel said.

'It might be more than bad luck,' Ramzi said.

Rebecca opened her laptop. 'Here they are,' she said. 'Spielman, Abigail and Yitzak, and opposite, Oren and Ester.'

Ramzi peered at the screen. Behind those sitting at the banqueting tables, people danced or stood and talked. Then men wore *kippahs*, including one of the waiters in a uniform of black shirt and trousers, captured pouring *mahia* into Spielman's glass. Abigail and Yitzak looked abstracted. Oren smiled, but Ester seemed to find her seat across from Spielman distasteful.

'It all seems innocent enough. Though we know the four guests left soon afterwards.'

'Yes. In this one, Oren has gone. Look, this is Spielman standing and addressing the table—not the hall. That's when Ester left. And look at that—Yitzak and Abigail are leaving, there in the background. But Spielman was certainly drinking—a waiter's refilling his glass.'

She closed the screen.

'Well at least you saved your photographs. I had better go and have a shower.'

Rachel opened the door and Rebecca hugged Ramzi as he left. He smiled with surprise. On the landing downstairs Oren and

Ester looked up at them. Ester's mouth dropped open and Oren winked.

*

After a shave, shower and repacking his clothes in the suitcase, Ramzi's phone jingled.

A message from Rashida lit up on his phone.

Did you sleep well?

Unsure if this was concern or mischief, he ignored it. Needing a good breakfast, he reached the roof terrace. Ester was the only guest there.

'Did you sleep well?' she asked.

'Wonderfully,' Ramzi replied. 'This sea-air.'

Why had she asked that rather than just a good morning? Was she insinuating he'd spent the night with the twins? Or had she put the scorpion in the bed as, at the very least, some sort of warning?

Convinced she'd given herself away, the appearance of Youssef broke his train of thought.

'Did you sleep well, Monsieur Ramzi?'

'Wonderfully. Coffee would be fine, thank you. If there is any.'

'If you want coffee, count on me!'

'May I join you?' Ramzi said, turning to Ester.

'Of course.'

After preliminaries regarding the final *hillula* celebrations, Ramzi came to the point.

'Back to our chat yesterday. Tell me: who cast the *jidwel*?'

Ester straightened in her chair.

'I recognised him as we waited for the flight to Marrakech. He was one of the pilgrims singing and dancing. I cannot describe my anger and the stress it put me under. I thought the taxi laid on by Riad Safsaf would be a perfect tonic until I discovered he was also travelling with me, and worse, staying at the same place. He sat at the front, talking on his phone most of the trip—to family and friends in Israel—a construction contract he'd signed the day before—around twenty million shekels was mentioned—he sounded so smug, I felt close to tears. For my grandfather's sake, I knew I had to confront him.'

'Him?'

'Isaac Spielman.'

'Spielman wrote the *jidwel*?'

'I am certain of it.'

'You mentioned your grandfather? What happened?'

'As I said, my family left for Israel in 1963. Two years later my grandfather was eighteen and conscripted to the Israeli Defence

Force, where he met my grandmother, also on compulsory service.'

'Yes, you briefly remarked women were also conscripted into the military.'

'My grandmother's family were from Meknès. They fell head-over-heels in love, and married. Soon after, my grandmother became pregnant—the baby was my father—and left the army. My grandfather had one year more to serve in the Infantry Brigade. Spielman was the platoon leader and gave my father a hard time. First, because he was new to Israel; second, because in Essaouira he descended from a *Tajer as-Sultan*. Spielman was, to put it politely, a bully.'

'So I gather. I know he had already changed his name to draw a veil over his Sephardic origins.'

'Which takes me to June 1967 and the Six Day War.'

'The Arab-Israeli conflict.'

'That's the one. The platoon fought in the Sinai desert, at the Battle of Umm Qatef. Three of the soldiers were wounded. My grandfather threw his automatic rifle to Spielman. The rifle had a fresh clip in it, and as platoon leader, he was supposed to provide cover. My grandfather ran and pulled two of the wounded to safety behind an abandoned Egyptian tank. But there was no cover. Where was the cover? He looked round and saw

Spielman had taken off. Still, he ran back to rescue the third, but after bringing him to safety my grandfather collapsed, fatally shot. Spielman magically reappeared, and when the medical corps arrived to evacuate the wounded, he claimed he had rescued the men. None of them were in a state to challenge him. And hey presto! He became a hero. As a result, his credentials were impeccable. War heroes and heroism are important to Israel.'

'But how did you find this out?'

'After recuperating from their wounds, the three soldiers visited my grandmother and told her the truth about what happened.'

'There was nothing they could do?'

'What, and embarrass the military?'

'I can see the problem.'

'As it happened, one of the soldiers became very friendly with my grandmother. Eventually they married and he adopted my father. They had other children, but he never forgot the courage of my grandfather.'

'Did Spielman know this?'

'He must have heard. Of course, Spielman often appeared in the media, so at home it always reminded us of the bravery of my grandfather in the face of battle, but also of Spielman's cowardice.'

'I imagine it was a shock to find him here.'

'I couldn't let matters pass. I paced the room, certain I had a duty to my family to make Spielman see we knew the truth about Umm Qatef. I knocked on his door and confronted him.'

'Valiant, like your grandfather. How did that turn out?'

'He laughed, and tried to deny it, saying he had never fought at Umm Qatef. But I told him who my grandfather was, and he snapped. He threatened to kill me if I mentioned it to anyone, especially his son Yitzak, who was joining him. Basically, I told him nothing could stop me. I went to leave, and he grabbed me by the hair, spun me round and slapped me.'

'Oh my God, how terrible!'

'I pushed him away and went to my room, shaking with rage. That night, I woke up and found the *jidwel* under the door.'

'I see. Now that you've put things in context, he could have been responsible. However, I heard you were together on the night of the *hillula*?'

'We went in a group, so unfortunately, it was difficult to avoid that. Besides, I was intrigued to see his children, but it became clear all was not as it seemed. Yitzak, a *refusenik*—and Abigail critical of his involvement in building settlements and Israel in general.'

'That's rather an understatement.'

'You know about all that?'

'Well—it kind of came up in conversation.'

'I see. Anyhow, at dinner, Spielman started talking about what a hero he'd been at the Battle of Umm Qater.' Her face icy with fury, Ester continued, 'I felt as if he had slapped me a second time—'

'It sounds as if he was trying to upset you on purpose—'

'Good morning! Have you heard we had good news?' Abigail said in a sing-song voice.

Typical, Ramzi thought. Anytime a conversation became intriguing someone bobbed up to cut it short.

'No—' Ester said.

'It seems the authorities have decided against an autopsy, as there was a doctor on the scene and to prevent a diplomatic incident during the *hillula*. Zak's gone off with Inspector Hassan to deal with the paperwork and arrange the burial.'

'What a relief for you both,' Ramzi said.

'Did the Inspector bring back our passports?'

'They're coming later.'

Ester stood up. 'Good news. Excuse me, but I have a legal matter to attend to and I'd like to visit Rabbi Haim Pinto's tomb before I leave tomorrow.'

'I'm off to pack,' Abigail said.

Together, they headed downstairs. Alone, Ramzi assessed the news. The decision not to hold an autopsy meant they could only speculate as to Spielman's cause of death. Was it natural causes after all, or in fact, murder?

Obviously, Spielman set out to taunt Ester at the *hillula* with his talk of heroics, as well as insulting Yitzak for being a *refusenik*—and, ironically, for cowardice—and Abigail for working toward peace for both Israelis and Palestinians. But was it enough of a provocation to lead to him being poisoned? Surely too, poison implied an element of premeditation, as the root of Glue Thistle was not a normal addition to a travel bag of toiletries?

'Thank you, Youssef.' Lost in thought, Ramzi had hardly been aware of the breakfast being laid in front of him.

'You're welcome.'

He had just poured a second cup of coffee, when he had a call.

'*Bonjour*, Ramzi! I imagine you heard the autopsy was refused. It's a bit annoying, as all the red tape will eat into the day I planned windsurfing. The official cause of death is a cardiac arrest,' Rashida added.

'Unfortunately, there was a doctor present when he died.'

'You are funny Ramzi. I still maintain he was poisoned.'

'Does it matter?'

'That a murder has been committed? Yes, it does,' Rashida said

'But proving it?'

'Well, was the scorpion in the bed by accident or design?'

'Well,' Ramzi said. 'As the sheets were so tightly tucked in, and the top opening covered by pillows, it seems unlikely that my friend would manage it alone. I think someone was trying to scare me off.'

'Who and why? We'll talk later. I just received a batch of forms to process.'

TWENTY

After the stories of the Holy Land, Ramzi walked aimlessly through the lanes, along the Avenue Istiqlal, into the gateway of Souk Jdid. As he did so, he found it inspiring to be amongst Jewish pilgrims for the *hillula*, Christian tourists and Muslims, the religions mixing together with mutual respect and honour, as it was once in Palestine. Turning again into Souk Laghzal, he jerked as a man ran up to him.

'Hello sir! Remember me? How is your wife? Do you still want the "elixir" we talked about?'

'Err—all is fine at the moment.'

'I see, sir. Problems with your girlfriend. If I may say, she looked a handful. I have something for that too.'

'Not today, but thank you.'

'It was a funny thing, sir. I talked to my colleagues in the market, and they said other people had been asking about *addad*.'

'The Glue Thistle?' Ramzi said.

'Correct. It was the day before you came to talk to me. Maybe your wife? *Ya* Brahim!'

A young man outside a further shop joined them.

'Brahim, tell him about the *addad*.'

'Yes, two women came and asked about poisons.'

'Though I am the local expert, as you know.'

'They bought some *addad*. Dried.'

'Not as effective as fresh—but still deadly.'

'Were they Moroccan? Can you describe them?' Ramzi asked.

'The women were tourists. Twins.'

Twins! Ramzi's head spun as he thanked the man and left. Were Rachel and Rebecca involved in Spielman's death? Had they put up a smokescreen about who they were?

Yet again—nothing was as it seemed. Wandering between mottled façades, the wind buffeted him in every direction, as did the riddle of Spielman's death. Reaching the square and seeing Yitzak sitting on the esplanade of the *Café de France*, he decided to play innocent.

'Hi Yitzak. How are things? Any news on the autopsy?' he said, joining him.

'Didn't you hear? It's been refused.'

'Diplomacy, I imagine.'

'Or maybe a simple case of natural causes?'

'Well, that too.'

'At least now you can pay off your debts,' Ramzi said.

'How did you know about that?'

'I heard you and your wife talking on the terrace last night.'

'The missing motive,' Yitzak laughed. 'Money.'

'You don't deny it?'

Yitzak leant forward and lowered his voice. 'Well as the case is officially closed, I might as well make a little confession. I killed my father.'

TWENTY-ONE

'How?' Ramzi asked. 'Was it a revolver, or with a candlestick?'

'I don't think you are taking me seriously.'

'I'm listening.'

'You were right about the money. I invested in a start-up. It seemed a sure-fired idea, but it went bust. I'd re-mortgaged the house, and had to withdraw part of the boys' college funds to keep a roof over our head.'

'Did your father know about this?'

'Not until the night of the *hillula*. He had drunk a lot of *mahia*. Then I told him, and asked if he could lend me some money for his grandsons' schooling.'

'What was his reaction?'

'He took the opportunity to publicly insult me, and Abigail. On he went: as a *refusenik* I was a coward, because of the bad investment I was a gambler, and Abigail was a traitor to Israel by supporting the Jewish Voice for Peace.'

'You left early?'

'Frankly, if he was such a hero and martyr he could find his own way back.'

'But you said you killed him—?'

For a moment Yitzak said nothing. A woman paid and, as she left, Ramzi noticed Poppy's elderly neighbour Émile Martin, sitting alone. A bottle of water in hand, he followed a wasp round his café table, then slammed down the glass, grinding it against the metal surface, with a flicker of a smile. Although Ramzi disliked wasps, its end startled him. Not even a benediction!

'Am I scaring you?' Yitzak said.

Brought back to the matter in hand, Ramzi shook his head. 'Not at all. I look forward to hearing how you did the murder.'

'My father had high pressure and angina attacks. Random ones.'

'Yes, I know. He had a small chest pain the morning he showed me round the Mellah.'

'Well, before we left for the *hillula* he asked Abigail to take his nitro pills in her bag, in case of a sudden angina attack. We reached the ceremony, and found a table in the ceremonial hall. When the celebrations began, I kept topping up his glass of *mahia*. It's strong stuff—'

'The waiter did too, from what I've seen. But go on.'

'As I said, we went back to the riad without him. We were tired and upset, and went straight to bed. I remembered about the pillbox, but thought, why should I care?'

'You didn't put it in his room?'

'No. Then, of course, the heavy meal and the *mahia* probably caused an angina attack as he went to bed, and led to the vomiting. He didn't have his pills. It must have all combined to trigger the heart attack.'

'You forgot about the diarrhoea. Dr Rashida suspected poison.'

'I think that's a bit far-fetched.'

'When I first saw him, he was clutching his stomach, not his chest.'

'That may be, but nothing can be proved without an autopsy. You saw what we saw—his heart stopped. If he'd had his angina pills, he'd have been here today.'

'Did you tell this to Inspector Hassani?'

'No. You see, when everyone left the room, I put the pillbox back.'

'On the nightstand—'

'You saw it? What now? Are you going to call the police?' 'Well, without an autopsy—'

'Exactly. I'm in the clear,' Yitzak smiled.

TWENTY-TWO

Settling on a lounger on the roof terrace, Ramzi was startled by a cacophony of adults and children shouting and crying, the sounds rising in eerie echoes from the courtyard shaft of the riad belonging to Poppy's neighbour, Émile Martin. Putting his book down, he crossed to the adjoining terrace wall but saw nothing, and although he picked up some French, the sea and gulls drowned the details.

Turning he saw Rachel and Rebecca hesitating at the doorway.

'There seems to be some drama going on next door.'

'Very likely,' Rachel shrugged. 'Sounds like a family torn apart.'

'We came to say my camera turned up,' Rebecca said. 'In the salon, by all accounts.'

'That's lucky.'

'Minus the memory card.'

'That's interesting. I imagine someone wanted it to hide evidence.'

'It could be.'

'I gather there's no autopsy? We'll never know if poison killed him or he died of natural causes.'

'If it was poison, who did the deed?' Rachel asked.

'Strangely enough, I was shopping for spices this morning and heard that twin sisters bought poison the day that Spielman died. Glue Thistle, also known as *addad*. The symptoms match.'

'I'm sure we aren't the only twin sisters in Essaouira,' Rebecca said.

'Maybe not, but you had the opportunity as you helped him back to the riad.'

'That's true, but no autopsy means no evidence. Why would we kill him?'

'Exactly. No motive,' Rachel said.

'I suppose it's the scientist in me, but I like problems to be solved. As you say, I can't do anything even if you do confess.'

The twins looked at each other. Rebecca nodded.

'Okay Ramzi. We'll come clean.'

'But not now. Later.'

'We're off to a cooking class.'

Speechless, his phone cut in.

'Hisham!

'How are you Mr. Ramzi? Are you feeling calm?'

'I think so.'

'There's an e-mail from Ryan.'

'Hold on a minute, I'll get back to you.'

*

In his room, Ramzi opened his laptop, and read Ryan's e-mail.

> *For some years now I have been with a bill recovery team called DebtPlan as I struggled to make payments on credit cards, loans etc. I pay DebtPlan an amount each month (using income / expenditure) and they distribute that amount accordingly depending on the size of the debt I can either add your debt to this over the next 24 months or pay immediately, but with 30% subtracted.*

Nothing was as it seems—the phrase rang in his head. Although he'd checked out Google Maps, zooming onto the modest terraced house, Kayla and her husband had serious debt issues. Looking back, he recalled the latest phones, iPads, designer clothes and handbags, plus the trips, such as to New York. They were clearly living beyond their means and that might explain it. Who knows, or who was he to judge?

Still, most facts fitted. As he and the police suspected, the robbery at Riad Waqi was staged as an insurance scam. The passport may well have been lost or stolen outside the riad, and prompted the idea. Yet maybe it wasn't. After all, judging by the moments of hesitation, Kayla hadn't banked on Ramzi organising a replacement document, forcing her to keep up the charade.

Even worse! Gallantly, Kayla promised to collect everyone's share to pay for their stay. That was a substantial amount. Had she and her husband decided to use this money to help pay off their debts, hoping Ramzi would quietly forget about it, whilst the rest of the Hen Party would be none the wiser? More unpleasant still, amongst those deceived would be Irene and Colleen—her own mother and sister!

Another jingle. Hisham.

'You can't feel sorry.'

Hisham the Mind Reader!

'Err—'

'They are cheating you out of money. Thirty per cent!'

As well as their own friends and family, Ramzi thought.

'You are right. This is a serious matter, I will write back.'

'I will read it Mr. Ramzi—'

Was that a veiled threat? He started typing in his best legalise.

Dear Ryan,

Without Prejudice.

We both agree that we do not want the matter to drag on. Unfortunately, there is little room to manoeuvre.

As the payment had not been honoured, the matter has had to be pursued through a Debt Recovery Agency who take a percentage of the amount retrieved. The legal costs to date (for which the defendant is liable) has already added an additional sum to the original amount due. To subtract a further 30% off this amount plus the other costs is not a satisfactory offer.

My preference is an immediate settlement. To resolve the situation, I would be prepared to allow for a 10% discount. In return, I will pay the other costs. A financial breakdown of these options is set down below.

Honour satisfied?

Calculations detailed, Ramzi pressed send. He waited but there was no call for changes from Hisham. The brief moment of tranquillity was shaken by a loud knock on the bedroom door.

'Mr.. Ramzi. We have a family arriving

tomorrow from Montpelier and need all the rooms. Would you like to pay your bill now or later?'

TWENTY-THREE

Ramzi had bought a one-way bus ticket to Essaouira—maybe a subconscious decision. Now, as Poppy needed the room, his departure had been decided for him. Cutting through the Medina, Ramzi trooped through the Bab Marrakech gateway, sad to be leaving Essaouira, an unsolved murder—and Rashida. Apart from a desk clerk, playing solitaire with black marble balls on a wooden base, the SupraTours ticket office was empty, so he swiftly bought a seat on the 11.15 the following morning.

About to retrace his steps, on the spur of the moment, Ramzi decided to trek east to the dune forest mentioned by the spice seller. Passing a hospital to his left, he instinctively navigated his way through low blocks of apartments to Avenue Attaif, that seemed to be the barrier between the dune forest and the city. Amidst the sour stench of decaying fruit and vegetables, a cow fed itself from an overturned dumpster. Skirting this, he crossed to a wide, candy-striped pavement edged by iron fencing painted green and gold. Which way now?

Nearby, a man sat on the pavement, beside a small metal dish holding a few dirham coins. Wound round the man's head was a grey cloth, and his beard was unkempt. His blue eyes were not unusual if he was from the north of Morocco. His *jellaba* and bare feet were caked with dirt.

'*Salam alay-kum. Ayn madkhal alhadiqa*?' Ramzi said.

The man looked at him and shook his head. It must be his accent, Ramzi thought. He switched to French.

'*Bonjour Monsieur. Où est l'entrée du parc?*'

No response. He must be a person who is either hard of hearing or deaf.

'*OÙ EST L'ENTRÉE DU PARC?*' Ramzi shouted.

Again, the man shook his head. Feeling a pang of compassion, Ramzi put a fifty dirham note in the dish, and stepped away.

'Ta, mate!'

Ramzi turned.

'*Ta, mate?*'

Standing, the man slipped the note into the *jellaba*'s pocket, and held out his hand. 'Josh.'

'Ramzi. I thought you were Moroccan.'

'Nah. I'm an Aussie. From Sydney. A place called Woolloomooloo.'

'How—?' Ramzi gestured at Josh's appearance.

'Long bloody story. Cheers anyway. I'm off to get a coldie. Catch you later.'

'Wait! Is there a gateway?'

The Aussie pointed southwards, unwound his turban, picked up his dish and ambled off to find that beer.

Fazed, Ramzi forged ahead. Finally, there it was—an arched gateway to the dune park.

Household garbage at the entrance to this eco-environment unsettled him. He followed a meandering pathway, dodging wild dogs, though most slept under the trees or in the shade of bushes on the dunes. Following a rough pathway, he recognized thuja and argan trees planted amongst the eucalyptus, tamaris and carob. Exchanging greetings with a herder grazing a flock of brown and white camels, Hisham's photo request figured in his mind. Rambling on, a goat appeared. Ahead a flamboyance of flamingos was a shimmer of pink across a small lagoon. Navigating the sandy earth, he saw spreading marigolds and beyond, spiny plants with purple flower-heads. Was it a Glue Thistle? Bending over, he began to scrape his hands around one, to see if he identified the root.

TWENTY-FOUR

Back at Riad Safsaf, Ramzi lurked in the salon, shooting out as Rachel and Rebecca came through the front door.

'Oh hello!'

'You weren't waiting for us, were you?'

'Goodness me, no. Just having a change of scenery. How was the cooking class?'

'Great fun!' Rachel said. 'We made lamb tagine with figs and apricots. It was delicious and quite eye-catching.'

'Food photography is a speciality of mine,' Rebecca explained.

'Poppy gave us our marching orders tomorrow. We just bought our ticket for Marrakech.'

'SupraTours.'

'Oh? So, did I. The 11.15.'

'Same bus as us! Good timing, as our work is almost done here.'

Ramzi couldn't believe his luck!

'I feel like celebrating. Let's finish off the *Tubi 60*. Bring a glass and join us.'

Ramzi followed them to their room.

'You may need this,' Rachel said, opening the *Tubi 60*.

'We do,' Rebecca chimed.

'Thank you.'

'Time to confess!' they both said in unison.

'I'm glad you are so cheerful about it.'

Rachel smiled. 'We are here for the reasons we said. Putting together an article on the "left behind" in Casablanca and another one on the *hillula*. But we were also investigating somebody else.'

'Isaac Spielman?' Ramzi speculated.

'No. Emilis Martinaitis.'

'Also known as Émile Martin.'

'Riad Safsaf's neighbour—the old man? What's so special about him? Because he changed his name? Spielman changed his surname to replace Knafo.'

'The name is Lithuanian. My grandmother knew him. They lived in the same village of Pakuonis. It is rarely mentioned, but during the Holocaust, ninety-six percent of the country's Jews—which was around 200,000 people at the time—were murdered in a matter of months. Ninety per cent near their homes by their neighbours, and mainly by collaborators—or co-operators may be a more correct term.'

'Not by Nazis?'

Rachel replied by shaking her head, and continued, 'There were less than 1,000 Nazis stationed there during the war, yet over 230 mass graves. In 1941, only 8,000 of the 220,000 Jewish community were alive, just a few months after the Nazi occupation. Usually the Nazis did the organizational part of the persecution, and monitored the killing. In practice, they tended to leave the dirty work to the Lithuanian Police Battalion, who were paramilitaries, local police and partisan squads.'

'The white-bands,' Rebecca said. 'Their name sounds so innocent, don't you think?'

'Well,' Ramzi said, 'I suppose, traditionally, white does symbolize purity and goodness—'

Rebecca's voice shook. 'Maybe that's how they justified rounding up the Jews, rounding up men, women and children, to take them to be executed?'

After a short silence, Ramzi said, 'Forgive me if this sounds morbid, but may I ask—taken where?'

'People need to remember—' Rebecca said, her hand trembling as she refilled her glass.

'Mostly to fields or forests,' Rachel replied.

'Taken by the police, partisans, the

white-bands, not Nazis?'

'The Gestapo often arrived by car afterwards.'

'How does all of this involve Émile Martin?' Ramzi asked.

'He was one of the Lithuanian white-band squads of about 120 men active in Garliava Rural District. Massacres had already happened in the small border towns such as Gargzdai, though we don't know if he was already involved in those. In mid-August, local policemen and the white-bands herded the Jews of Garliava and neighbouring villages, including our grandmother's family from Pakuonis, to the town synagogue. Between August 28th and August 31st or perhaps September 2nd, the police and the white-bands forced several dozen men from the synagogue to walk to the valley close to the village of Rinkūnai, about a kilometre east, to dig a ditch, allegedly for drainage. Knowing the trench's purpose, the men refused.'

'Just like that?

'At the time, it seems nothing was clear-cut. The Chief of Police, Juozas Stankevičius, of the Rural District tried to maintain order and restrain the more active antisemites. Criminal charges for beating Jews and looting their property had been introduced against any white-bands responsible,' Rachel said.

'Later, that same Chief of Police was transferred because of this—' Rebecca added.

'So, local police brought several dozen of the Lithuanian men left in Garliava, who dug a trench, fifty to sixty metres long, two metres wide and one-and-a-half metres deep. On the day of the massacre, paramilitaries were selected from the 3rd Company 1st Lithuanian Police Battalion in the nearby city of Kaunus, and taken in two buses to Garliava. The buses stopped at the synagogue where the Jews were held. These policemen and white-bands ordered the Jews outside, forcing them to walk to the site of the execution.'

'Seventy-three men, 113 women and sixty-one children, including our grandmother's younger sister and brother, her father, her mother and grandmother—' Rebecca said, her tone acid.

Rachel took a gulp of the *Tubi 60*. 'There they were divided, and one by one the groups sent to the edge of trench.'

'Men first. To be shot in the back,' Rebecca added.

'Cowardly, but more anonymous,' Ramzi said.

'It was and, even worse, some of the white-bands knew the villagers. As the first Jews fell, the next victims had to push the bodies into the ditch before they were murdered and so on, until the last person standing. Pit killings they called it. The execution started in the late afternoon and continued into the night, some of the policemen finishing off the injured by torchlight. Afterwards, the 3rd Company returned to Kaunus to drink beer in a bar, while the white-bands rounded up local villagers to fill in the trench.'

'So, there were no Nazis at the massacre at all?' Ramzi said, surprised.

'Not that any witness recalls. My grandmother was thirteen at the time, in one of the last groups. She'd recognised Martinaitis among the executioners, and when they raised their guns, she threw herself on the bodies. In the twilight, no one really noticed.'

'When the shooting finished, she crawled out into the bushes and stayed put until the men finished burying the bodies.' Rebecca said.

'After everyone left, our grandmother began to walk eastwards into Russia. Two nights later she slept just inside the gateway of a cottage, planning to leave at dawn. When she woke, it was already morning and a woman stood over her. "My poor girl," the woman said and took her inside. She was a schoolteacher, and she hid her.

'Then one day, about two years later, the teacher didn't return from the school. Militia stormed the house, and my grandmother was taken prisoner. First, they sent her to the Jewish ghetto in Kaunus, and later, to the concentration camp at Stutthof. By some miracle she survived and after liberation was classed as a displaced person, and sent to Palestine.'

'The point being, she recognised one of the partisans who was involved in the executions. He was from her village, Pakuonis,' Rebecca concluded.

Ramzi recalled how Émile had violently killed the wasp in the *Café de France*, but tried to be diplomatic. 'If you are correct, Émile Martins—or Martinaitis—is over ninety years old. Isn't it time to draw a line in the sand?'

The twins looked at him.

'Playing devil's advocate, of course' he added.

'They have a nick-name in Lithuanian for them. *Zydsaudys.* Jew shooters. That's how common it was. And he was one of them.' Rachel said.

'No way does Time lessen the guilt of his murders,' Rebecca said. 'Why should old age give him protection? He was a teenager in the peak of physical health and devoted his energy to helping murder the men, women and children from his own village. Neighbours! Friends!'

'Ramzi, we owe an obligation to the victims and families to hold him accountable. To our own family. He's lived his life to the full, and cut other's lives short.'

'Every testimony helps fight against Holocaust denial and distorting what happened. Our only worry is that he probably won't come to trial. Extradition procedures, court delays, his age—everything conspires against it.'

'I understand your point. But why now? How can you even be sure it's him?

'We contacted Operation Last Chance, linked to the Wiesenthal Centre. They offer 25,000 American dollars for information—of course, the money is of no interest.'

'Rebecca and I went back to the Pakuonis. We went to see if the priest knew the murderer's family.'

'Pretty church. White and red brick.'

Rolling her eyes, Rachel moved on. 'It turned out Martinaitis' sister was still alive. The priest took us there. She hadn't seen her brother since the middle of the war, but she had a photograph of him. It had gone yellow with time, but the image was clear. I took a picture of it. Then, as were about to leave, she called us back. After the war, she had received a postcard from Algeria.'

'His sister rummaged around, and found it in a drawer. Sidi-Bel-Abbès. It had a postmark dated December 1946.'

'Had he written anything?'

'It said: *I hope you all survived. In my thoughts, always. E.*'

'Isn't Sidi Bel Abbès where the Foreign Legion was based until after Algerian Independence?' Ramzi asked.

'Spot on.' She opened her laptop. 'Here is the scan I took with my phone.'

The card showed a gateway with legionnaires in white képi caps, and an Algerian in a white tunic and a burnous cloak. Beneath the photo read, *Caserne de la Légion Étrangère 1er Régiment.* Obscuring the top right of the picture, was a watermarked red stamp, showing an indistinct view through a Moorish arch with the words *POSTE ALGÉRIE* and the letters RF, that Ramzi presumed to stand for *République Française.*

'We guessed the card itself was a message, that he managed to get to France, maybe Marseille, to join the Foreign Legion. A perfect place to disappear—no questions asked. The war helped, as lots of people had lost their documents. To help integrate quicker, recruits are given a new identity: as they were required to enlist as an *anonymat*, with their birth date a month or so out. It was a five-year contract, but after three years, with good behaviour, he could apply for French nationality, which he did.

'It took some work, but we found the name of a recruit, Emile Maarten. He put his nationality as Dutch. It seemed too close to Emilias Matinaitis to be chance. Then we discovered the *livret matricule*, the Legion's military file. Emile Maarten, served under the given name Édouard Marat, with a time-line which seemed to fit. He applied for nationality as Martin, a common French surname, so difficult to track down.'

'It might be the *Tubi 60*, but my head's spinning—if it wasn't for the circumstances, I'd be impressed at the subterfuge. And he left the *Légion Étrangère*?'

'Not quite. First, he was on active service in Indo-China, including at the battle of Phu Tong Hoa. He must have sent the postcard from Algeria before being deployed to the Orient. After his five-year service he returned to Algeria, received his nationality and went on to marry a Frenchwoman. After Algeria declared Independence from France, they crossed to Morocco, settling in Casablanca. When his wife died, he moved to Essaouira.'

'The French Embassy confirmed Émile Martin's address. From that, we found this guest house next door.'

'That explains the photographs from the roof terrace, the morning I arrived.'

Rebecca smiled, took her laptop from the nightstand, and opened it. 'I did take one of the cat. But, yes—we had to make sure. There is the photo Martainitis's sister gave us of him as a young man. We had a digital facial aging done to it on the computer. You can see a distinct similarity. Look—'

Ramzi leant toward the computer screen. A good looking, fresh-faced young man. Alongside, the image of the ninety-year old man next door.

'The police came this morning and confiscated his passport.'

'They will terminate his residence permit.'

'Will he be extradited?' Ramzi asked.

'These things take time. Statutes of limitations complicate matters.'

'The state of limitation in France and Lithuania is 30 years, and Lithuania has no agreement with Israel.'

'Otherwise, he could be prosecuted in Israel under the Nazis and Nazi Collaborators Punishment Law, for crimes against the Jewish people, crimes against humanity and war crimes.'

'The irony being, that only three men out of the hundreds of *Zydsaudys* have attempted to be prosecuted in Lithuania, but health reasons stopped even them serving any sentence.'

'So, he is free,' Ramzi said, flatly.

'He will never be, especially now. Didn't you hear the commotion? His secret is out. His family know now. Their life will never be the same.'

'So, it wasn't you that bought the poison?'

The twins looked at each other. Rebecca opened her camera bag and took out a small pouch.

'This?' she said. 'We were so angry when we found him. We wanted revenge. Even though we had alerted the authorities in Israel, we wondered if nothing would happen. It's easy to drop down onto his terrace, force him to take the poison, and avenge all the people he murdered.'

'We had it all planned,' Rachel said. 'Then we thought, or rather, I thought, we would be no better than him. Murder, by its very definition, is an unlawful killing.'

'I agree,' Ramzi nodded. 'It is not up to the individual to exercise justice. How can it be ethical to murder when we consider it ethical to stick by the law?'

'Well, in this case I have my doubts,' Rebecca said, her tone sombre.

TWENTY-FIVE

'I have to go tomorrow,' Ramzi said, a glass of white wine in hand. 'Poppy needs the rooms for other guests.'

'Leaving a poisoner at large,' Rashida remarked.

'Not quite. Yitzak confessed!'

They were back on the roof terrace of the *Taros*. Rashida listened and, in the end she said, 'Angina is a symptom, not a disease or condition. However, this symptom is a sign of coronary artery disease, which means his father could have had a higher risk of a heart attack. Maybe that's what happened. Don't forget the stress that day—Spielman's issues with his son and daughter-in-law, Oren asking for work and of course, going back to his roots. Plus, the violent reaction to the poison. However, the symptoms are all wrong.'

'Maybe it was a bluff? Yitzak killed him, but thought by telling me about the pills, it would rule him out.'

'Or rule out Abigail?'

'On top of that, the twins Rebecca and Rachel bought a packet of powdered Glue Thistle.'

'Did they confess as well?'

'I challenged them. I was in the souk and the CAPM contact we spoke to had found out twin sisters had bought the poison from a colleague.'

'Maybe they wanted to bump off your wife too?' Rashida smiled.

Not rising to the bait, Ramzi said, 'In fact, they found a murderer.'

He retold the twins' story.

Rashida sighed. 'Well, it's certainly been an exciting day—or few days, for you.'

'I'd hoped for something more relaxing. The only quiet time was wandering through the dune forest—but even then, I was really looking for Glue Thistle. I tried to dig one up to see the root.'

'I hope you washed your hands. Listen, why not come with me to Sidi Koulki, just south of here, for three nights. Separate rooms, naturally.'

'Naturally,' Ramzi said.

'Then we'll drive back to Marrakech.'

'Separate cars?'

'Naturally.'

Yet, to allay a surge of anxiety, Ramzi said, 'I forgot to tell you the story of the beggar by the park.'

Nevertheless, he started tripping over the pronunciation of Woolloomooloo. Rashida, already amused, was now more so.

'Have another glass of wine,' she said.

Flustered, a diversion saved him—

'Over there! Is that a falcon?'

Rashida looked up. 'Yes, I think it is. Eleonora's Falcon. The birds nest over there on Mogador Island before wintering in Madagascar.'

'Sounds ideal. Was that something in its beak? I thought most birds only hunted in daylight.'

'Well, there's still over an hour to sunset. I saw it too, perhaps it was a passerine? After capturing them, they tear off their wing and tail feathers, then store them alive in rock holes and cracks on the island. Later on, they kill them for feeding.'

Ramzi shuddered. 'How gruesome. I seem to be learning a lot about birds here. Abigail was telling me about seagulls and I joked—'

He stopped. Of course! Nothing was as it seemed!

'Ramzi, are you okay?'

'I think I know who murdered Spielman.'

TWENTY-SIX

A hush had fallen over Riad Safsaf. Ramzi stirred, opened his eyes, reaching for his watch. Almost ten o'clock! In record time, he showered, dressed and packed his toiletries and pyjama shorts. Outside his room, piles of sheets and towels littered the landing.

Change-over day.

Downstairs, he did a double-take. Poppy was hugging Ester!

Bemused, Ramzi said, 'Good morning. Is this the way you say goodbye to all your guests?'

'Ester is not going to put a claim against the ownership of the riad,' Poppy said. 'What a relief!'

'That's very civil of you Ester. What changed your mind?'

'Remember yesterday? I made a final visit to Haim Pinto's tomb.' Ester said.

'Of course.'

'Guess what happened? As I left, I saw a chameleon. It ran down the light-yellow wall of the mausoleum, into some weeds between the graves and changed colour.'

'And—?'

'I knew it was a sign from the *tzaddik*, to change my mind, to change the riad's ownership, and move on.'

That's scientific logic for you, Ramzi thought.

'Is everyone leaving?'

'Left,' Poppy said, smiling. 'We have new guests coming this evening. Abigail and Yitzak just took off by taxi to Casablanca to accompany Spielman's body to Israel. Via Frankfurt I think. I didn't charge for his room; should I have? Anyhow, luckily I just had time to tell them.'

'Tell them what? About the room?'

'No. It seems something contagious is going around. Poor Émile next door.'

'What happened?'

'The housekeeper went in this morning and found him dead.'

'Dead! How?'

'The same stomach bug that killed *Monsieur* Spielman. They found evidence of sickness and diarrhoea. The housekeeper thinks he tried to go for help, as she found him at the bottom of the stairs. Apart from the fact the steps are tiled, they are so steep in these riads, and at his age—'

'Do Rachel and Rebecca know?

'Why would it interest them? Besides they rushed off at the crack of dawn on the 6.30 bus to Marrakech. I thought they were going later, on the 11.15 they said, but they left a note with the front door key outside the office. Right—here's your receipt, with your company's tax number as you requested.

Ramzi barely heard, but thanked her. Émile Martin dead together with Rachel and Rebecca's hasty departure. Surely it was no coincidence?

'Has Oren gone yet?' Ramzi asked.

'No. He may be staying a little longer. Not at Safsaf though—'

'I'd like to see him before I go—'

Youssef came down the stairs. 'I was just tidying up the wooden ladder on the terrace. One of the guests must have moved it. 'Would you like breakfast sir?'

'Actually, I was wondering if you could show me any of your enchanting paintings that might be for sale? It's a present for a friend of mine.'

Youssef grinned. 'Certainly, sir. Is that okay, *Madame* Poppy? I thought *Monsieur* Ramzi had excellent taste.'

'Yes, but we have a lot to do today. Remember that you forgot to strip a room before the *hillula*.'

'That wasn't my fault *Madame* Poppy. The guest had made up the bed and when—' Youssef began.

'Whether it was or not—'

'You can trust me *Madame* Poppy. This way, sir.'

To Ramzi's surprise, Youssef led him from the riad, up the tunnelled lane. Veering right, he unlocked a metal door, giving directly to a flight of stairs. Opening another door, Youssef waved Ramzi in.

At the threshold, he felt a jolt, like a change of energy. Inside, despite the light fluttering through a high window, the overriding sensation was one of darkness.

'Welcome to my atelier. What size painting are you looking for sir?' Youssef crossed to the canvases propped against a wall, lifting up a large painting. 'This was my dream period,' he said, revealing lurid fish, multiple human eyes, animals baring teeth and fingers with castanets. It resembled a nightmare.

'Something easy to transport would be better. You must be glad the *hillula* is over?'

'Why glad? It is a great blessing in Essaouira to have the Jewish community from all over the world coming to honour the *tzaddik* Rabbi Haim Pinto.'

'Of course. It's just that Rebecca showed me a photo of the group at Spielman's table at the dinner on the night he died, and I recognised one of the waiters. Wearing a *kippah*.'

'Who was that, sir?'

'It was you, Youssef. Is that why you always wear a baseball cap? To keep your head covered in a Jewish tradition?'

'Is that the best you can do, sir? A lot of Moroccans wear baseball caps.'

'Even on duty at a riad?'

'*Madame* Poppy is very relaxed about how I dress. Try again, sir.'

'I also recall your fingernails seemed dirty as if you had been handling earth. I wondered if that was from digging up a Glue Thistle plant?'

'Glue Thistle?'

'*Addad*. It is more potent freshly picked, and alcohol makes the poison take effect more quickly.'

Youssef narrowed his eyes. 'I don't understand. There was no autopsy and now you make these accusations. Only a few minutes ago *Madame* Poppy said that *Monsieur* Émile died the same way.'

'I do not know for certain how he died. However, I trust the judgement of the doctor who tried to save Spielman.'

'Is that all you have against me?'

'No. You also have every Saturday—the Sabbath—as a day off.'

Youssef laughed. 'A lot of people have Saturday off.'

'Still, it was strange that you were absent from work the day after Spielman died.'

'Of course, these are just guesses.'

Ramzi changed tack. 'Of course. But you are an artist, and poisoning Spielman was very creative.'

Youssef smiled. 'In what way?'

'You must have planned it at the last minute. I suspect you dug up a Glue Thistle plant—I know you can find them in the dune forest just outside the town—and grated the root. I recall Spielman saying how much he liked the complimentary date left on the nightstands. I think you removed some almond paste, and packed in the poison. Only a small amount was needed. You waited until everyone left for the *hillula*, put the poisoned date in place, and went directly to the celebration, already changed into your waiter outfit. Whilst you were serving, you kept refilling Spielman's glass with *mahia*—as I said, alcohol gives a faster reaction. You took the chance that without the baseball cap no one would recognise you. Quite ingenious.'

Youssef looked smug. 'Few people notice a waiter, or the help in general, sir.'

'I saw the medjoul date was missing. The master stroke being, you were off work the next day. So, the list of suspects didn't include you. The room was closed but next day, a date was back on the nightstand, as if Spielman had left it untouched.'

'You have a good eye for detail, sir. When I left school, I helped out in a spice shop. You can learn a lot there. I knew *addad*—the Glue Thistle as you call it—was a deadly poison. Afterwards I found work at people's riads. They paid more money and it helped me sell my paintings to guests.'

'And it was you who took the camera.'

'I heard *Madame* Rebecca say they had photographs of the dinner. I took the camera and pulled out the memory card.'

'Not knowing they had been downloaded to her laptop. Nonetheless, it just lacks the motive. Was it feelings of envy? You were beside his breakfast table on the roof terrace when he bragged about how wealthy he was.'

Youssef ran his tongue over his upper lip. 'I am a famous painter, but I work in a riad. Spielman talked about how rich he had become in Israel, and I should have had that chance too. He held me back.'

'Held you back? How? Did you know him?'

'Oh yes, sir. Every day since the day I was born, all I heard were the two words Isaac Knafo, Isaac Knafo, Isaac Knafo. Then last week, he arrives at where I work, boasting about his money and success. If he hadn't filled out the Police Registration Card with his original name, I wouldn't have known.'

'It was certainly a coincidence.'

'Was it, sir? The *tzaddik* Haim Pinto is famous for helping people in mysterious ways.'

'Then you did know Spielman?' Ramzi asked, surprised.

'By name. When he was young and there was still a Jewish Community in Essaouira, he befriended my father. He dared him to do things, like steal a biscuit or throw a rotten vegetable at someone without them seeing. My father did those things, because he was scared of being bullied by him if he didn't.

'Then one day, Spielman dared him climb up the scaffolding on one side of a fishing trawler pulled onto the dry dock for repairs. The owner spotted him and went up after him, but my father crossed the deck, hung off the other side, and jumped. He hurt his leg, but managed to get away. He was a kid. It wasn't broken but, in time, it grew crooked and shorter than his other leg.

'Then the *Aliyah* Emissaries came, persuading them to emigrate to Israel. My grandparents sold our house and furniture.

They were ready to leave at dawn, outside the gateway by the Mellah. When the officials saw my father's limp they refused to take him. My grandparents couldn't leave him. What hope then, with a crippled son?'

Ramzi recalled he and Spielman saw the old man with a limp in the Mellah—was that Youssef's father? And Spielman's reaction—was it, remorse? In any event, Youssef's family seemed to be amongst the 'left behind'.

'My family had sold their house for next to nothing. A Moroccan Muslim bought it, to rent out. They had to take rooms in it. Rooms in their own house. A humiliation, don't you think? All the house was rented, but instead of my family of seven living there, now they shared it with four families and over twenty people. There were arguments all the time between my family and the other tenants. The landlord did no upkeep, and soon the property started to deteriorate.

'My father never recovered from a sense of guilt. Guilt and bitterness. As he grew older he started drinking. *Mahia*, too much *mahia*. All I heard about was Isaac Knafo and how he destroyed the family with that stupid dare. Isaac Knafo this, Isaac Knafo that. All my life. And look at what happened—he arrives for the *hillula*! I find he was a military hero, I find he was very rich. Of all the riads in

Essaouira, he's staying at Riad Safsaf. That is more than a coincidence, don't you think?

'Well now, are you going have me arrested? I don't have any regrets. My father, he wept like a child when I told him.'

Ramzi considered everything he had heard. 'As there wasn't an autopsy, it is just presumed Spielman died of over indulgence or food poisoning, leading to a heart failure. The body is already on its way back to Israel. The case is closed as far as the authorities are concerned.'

'Maybe I committed the perfect crime? As you said, I am a creative person. Also, I think the *tzaddik* Haim Pinto was watching over me. Apart from my father, look how I made *Monsieur* Yitzak and *Madame* Abigail so happy. Now, getting back to business, sir. Does this small painting of a scorpion interest you?'

EPILOGUE

Relegated to the back, as Rashida's windsurf board bag lay diagonally from the front seat to the rear, they set off to Sidi Koulki. Straining at the seatbelt, Ramzi leant forward and, competing with the noise of the engine, told Rashida about his morning with Youssef at his studio.

'Loathing is as good a motive as any. As for his father, a growth plate fracture of the tibia, I expect.'

'Growth plates?'

'Growth plates are at the end of certain bones that allow a child to grow. It's the weakest part of a child's skeleton. If not treated after an accident, they interrupt normal development—it's called growth arrest—causing a bone to grow unevenly and become crooked. This is probably what happened to Youssef's father. Two generations ago, medical costs were high and healthcare was poor. That said, if he'd had an X-Ray, the growth plate fracture might not have shown up, so probably, the injury would not be seen as serious. In adults, it's just thought of as a sprain to the ligaments. By the way—'

'Yes?'

'I could only get a double room. I hope that's alright—?'

As Ramzi's face reddened, his phone jingled.

'Hisham! How are you?'

'We have a new problem at the riad! Latifa—'

'Sorry Hisham, you are breaking up—!'

GLOSSARY

Abba—Father.

Addad—Glue Thistle (*Atractylis gummifera L.)* A poisonous thistle, often fatal, common in the Mediterranean region but frequently used in alternative medicine.

Aliyah—Hebrew for "ascent" or "going up. Jewish traditional views travelling to the Land of Israel as an ascent, both geographically and metaphysically.

Anonymat—An anonymous identity.

Aron ha kodesh—Holy Ark.

Bimah—The raised platform in the synagogue from which the Torah is read and services are led.

Five Pillars of Islam—the declaration of faith, prayer, pilgrimage to Mecca, alms-giving, and fasting.

Haganah—Zionist military organization representing the majority of Jews in Palestine from 1920 to 1948.

Halanat há'met— 'Leaving the dead overnight.' The Torah prohibits this, and commands a body be bried as soon after death as possible, preferably on the same day.

Hen Party—Bachelorette Party.

Hijab—Head covering worn by some Muslim women.

Hillula—Jewish pilgrimage to venerate the anniversary of the death of a great *tzaddik*.

Jidwel—A piece of paper with writing comprising a spell.

Kippah—A small round head covering worn by males.

Krav Maga—Literal meaning from Hebrew is 'contact combat'. A martial art developed for the Israel Defense Forces (IDF) from techniques such as judo, karate boxing and wrestling.

Ma'abarot—Tent cities converted into transition camps for immigrants. Around 80 per cent of the residents were Jewish migrants and refugees from the Middle East and North Africa.

Mahia—Moroccan-Jewish alcoholic drink distilled from date or figs.

Melkia—An informal document testifying ownership in the archaic Moroccan system that existed before the creation of the Land Register and official deeds system.

Mellah—Jewish quarter of a town or city in Morocco.

Nakba—Arabic for 'the disaster', 'catastrophe', or 'cataclysm' now known as the Palestinian Catastrophe, referring to the systematic destruction of the Palestinian society and homeland in 1947-1949 by Zionist military forces and the permanent displacement of several hundred thousand Palestinian Arabs, and including several massacres.

Neve Tzedek—A wealthy, exclusive district of Tel Aviv.

Oleh—Jewish migrant to Israel

Refusenik—In Israel the term is applied to conscientious objectots, Israeli soldiers or reservists who refuse to serve in the Occupied Palestinian Territories.

Riad—a traditional courtyard house in Morocco.

Shoura—A spell.

Skhina—A type of ragout of beef with potatoes chickpeas and seasoned with saffron and spices for the Sabbath

Sqala—An artillery platform built on the defensive walls of the port and town.

Talmud—the primary source of Jewish religious law and Jewish theology. A centrepiece of Jewish cultural life, it was the foundation of all Jewish thought and aspirations, and a guide to daily life.

Teshuva—To repent.

Toujjar as-Sultan—A group of ten Jewish merchants ennobled by the Sultan from 16th century endowed with fiscal benefits and under protection of the administration. Each *Tajer as-Sultan* (singular) was the gifted a house, two soldiers and two black African slaves. The title was passed from father to son.

Torah—The compilation of the first five books of the Hebrew Bible, name the books of Genesis, Exodus, Leviticus, Numbers and Deuteronomy.

Tzaddik—A highly learned and esteemed rabbinic leader often known as a 'saint' in North Africa.

White-Bands—Lithuanian paramilitary battalions (*Tautinio darbo apsaugos batalionas*) or TDA organised in June September 1941 by the Provisional Government of Lithuanian on the onset of Operation Barbarossa, when the Nazis invaded the Soviet Union. Members of the TDA were known by many names such as Lithuanian auxiliaries, policemen, white-bands, nationalists, rebels, partisans, or resistance fighters. TDA was intended as basis for the future independent Lithuanian Army, but soon it was taken over by Nazi officials and reorganized into the Lithuanian Auxiliary Police Battalions. The original TDA eventually became the 12th and the 13th Police Battalions. These two units took an active role in mass killings of the Jews in Lithuania.

ACKNOWLEDGEMENTS

The following were key to the background research for this novel.

www.annefrank.org

Christison, K&B. 2009 *Palestine in Pieces, Graphic perspectives of the Israeli Occupation.* Pluto Press, London.

Eisenberg, D. 2007. *Autopsy. How do we balance respecting the dead with the need to help the living?* October. www.aish.com

Elmaleh, R & Ricketts, G. 2012. *Jews under Moroccan Skies. Two thousand years of Jewish life.* Gaon Books, Santa Fe.

www.essaouira.nu

The Holocaust Atlas of Lithuania. www.holocaustatlas.lt

jewishvoiceforpeace.org

Kaleel, M. 1920. *When I was a boy in Palestine.* Harrap, London.

Lakdar, O. *Mogador Judaïca. Dernière génération d'une histoire millénaire.* Ed. Géographique.

Levin, L. 2011. *Jewish Agency. We discriminated against North Africans. This week in Haaretz 1949.* Haaretz.

Mor, S. 2007. *"Tell My Sister to Come and Get Me Out of Here"— A Reading of Ableism and Orientalism in Israel's Immigration Policy (The First Decade).* Disability Studies Quarterly, Vol.27, 4.

Pappe, I. 2013. *The Ethnic Cleansing of Palestine.* One World, London.

Sa'di H & Abu-Lughod L. 2007. *Nakba. Palestine 1948, and Claims of Memory.* Columbia University Press, New York.

https://en.wikipedia.org/wiki/Safsaf_massacre

Next in the Ramzi Murder Mystery Series

SHADOWS OF MEKNÈS

A grisly tale of another B&B in Marrakech appears prophetic after Ramzi hears plans for Riad Waqi from his manager Hisham. Alarmed, Ramzi travels north to join Dr Rashida visiting relatives in Meknès, taking up an invite to stay with the Jeandels at their vineyard nearby. Yet despite the tranquil setting, a hit-and-run, inconsistencies in the way the owner died, family disputes over producing a premium vintage partnered with an American wine critic or selling land entangled by tribal claims, culminate in another death. Was it just one more accident—or one more murder? Ramzi and Rashida try to uncork the truth, but a further mystery is afoot—why is Ramzi's housekeeper Latifa on strike and acting bizarrely?

Printed in Dunstable, United Kingdom

67355168R00133